What's in your noggin?

Who knows what primitive, terrible, twisted ideas and impulses are fizzing away in the strange chemistry sets we call people's brains?

Lies! Power grabs! Lust! Rivalries! Vendettas! Avarice! Secret crushes! Grudges, too, and everybody's messianic sense of mission are all in a day's work when people share a grand pre-war co-op building in Brooklyn.

Psychologist Michael Levine finds himself forced to investigate the dire, baffling goings-on in his building while navigating a tricky labyrinth of patients, neighbors, cops, a possible new girlfriend and his own randy, tormented mind.

At last – a salute to the gallant fighting men and women of America's co-ops and condos: game on!

Out of Order

NORMAN SCHREIBER

TOPQUARK PRESS
New York · London · Mars · Oort Cloud

OUT OF ORDER

A Topquark Press Book • First Edition • January 2012

This is a work of fiction. Names, characters, incidents derive from the author's imagination or are used fictitiously. Any resemblance to real persons, living or dead, is coincidental.

Cover Design by Sue Beal
Island Information Services • Key Largo

Cover illustration by Michael Fusco
www.michaelfusco.com

Interior Layout by Lighthouse24

ISBN-10: 1892881373
ISBN-13: 978-1-892881-37-3

TOPQUARK PRESS books are published by
TOPQUARK PRESS, PO Box 1801, FDR Station, New York, NY 10150 USA.

www.topquarkia.com

For Debbi, my cosmic love

ONE

Caution — Wet Floor

New York City napped until Andre Castellano's scream shook it awake. Castellano, a porter at the Olmsted Court apartment house, was in the building's basement. He had been dragging fat, green, stuffed garbage bags from the trash compactor room. He already had rummaged through the piled magazines and newspapers for a copy of that day's newspaper. The best he could find was a pristine, unread copy of the previous day's *New York Times*, dated April 23, 1982.

Bulging bag in each hand, Castellano sang "New York, New York" as he worked.

The compactor seemed to hum in harmony. But then it started to sputter. It was choking on some chunky morsel again.

Wondering when the co–op would buy a new compactor or, at least, fix this one, Castellano dropped the bags.

There are two kinds of problems, he thought. Most happen when things are not what they seem. The rest are because things are what they seem.

He scrambled to the compactor's base and threw a switch. The machinery's whining and coughing stopped. The compactor's pressing plate was stalled by the contents of a white plastic bag. Andre's hand closed tightly on the bag. Something felt wrong – and wet. His hand jerked open. Blood was on his hand. Blood painted the inside of the compactor.

The plastic bag had been torn open, and Andre saw its contents – a portion of a human torso. Peeking out from beneath was the head of the decedent, Herman Matterweil, president of the co-op. Herman's eye seemed to gaze right at the porter.

That's when Andre screamed. And that's when he ran to the super.

Upon hearing the news, Calvin Birmingham, the building superintendent, called 911 and the Police dispatcher directed a patrol car to Olmsted Court on Eastern Parkway in Brooklyn. News gathering organizations found their nostrils dilating when they heard the first call on their police band scanners.

The second call was even juicier. It came from the police officer sent to investigate. Portable two-way radio in hand, he was calling in from Olmsted Court's basement.

"It's awful," he screamed. "It's awful."

He started to retch.

A female voice from headquarters broke in. "Officer, tell us what's going on."

"A corpse."

"Male or female?"

"It's in pieces. It's cut into pieces. Oh God."

"Okay officer, take it easy. Now carefully describe everything for me."

The *New York Post's* City Editor crouched by the police scanner in his office. He looked like a farmer whose prayers for rain had been answered.

"What's to describe," said the cop. "It's a human body cut up like a chicken. Forget the ambulance. Send an erector set. Send a screwdriver."

The newspaper city editors, the radio news assignment editors, the television news assignment editors wrote the information down, and hollered or made phone calls or picked up the microphones from their own two-way radios and sent reporters and news teams careening toward Olmsted Court.

Sergeant Bernard Moscowitz was just maneuvering his green Pontiac toward the Flatbush Avenue exit of the Manhattan Bridge when he heard the second call on the police radio. He knew the third call would be for him, and it was.

Some jokers at the precinct house had taken to calling him the "Jewish cop" because he had his father's name. Others called him "schwartzer" because he had his mother's pigmentation.

Moscowitz had black hair, a neatly-trimmed, black mustache that extended just beyond his lips, a long diagonal scar on his neck, a slight paunch and a well-developed upper torso.

The scar always reminded Moscowitz that it was dangerous to be dumb and smart to be lucky.

Years ago when he still was in uniform, he was sent to a marital dispute call. Moscowitz's efforts to cool the situation failed. The husband grew increasingly incoherent

3

and abusive. The wife's fear-filled screams grew shriller. When Moscowitz managed to slap the cuffs on the husband, both husband and wife went silent. Moscowitz relaxed, and the wife snatched a carving knife from the stove and lunged for the cop. Moscowitz sensed the blur of movement from the corner of his eye, and tried to avoid the slash.

The knife did catch him in the neck; but his dodge spared him the humiliation of wearing a coroner's tag on his toe. With a beefy left hand pressing against the bleeding wound, he went into a crouch and butted the wife in the belly and then connected with a solid right to the jaw.

Upon release from the hospital, Moscowitz decided to practice caution whenever possible.

After he reported his find to the super, Andre knocked on Michael Levine's door for help. Levine, a psychotherapist, was one of the few shareholders who regularly said hello to Andre as if he meant it.

When Michael opened the door, he saw an agitated Andre Castellano, just repeating the phrase "Mr. Matterweil" over and over.

"No," said Michael patiently, "Mr. Matterweil isn't here."

Andre greeted this assertion with frantic arm waving and shouting. Suddenly he reached forward and tugged Michael out of the doorway and into the waiting freight elevator. Like a new Charon, the porter silently steered the car down to the basement.

Michael considered explaining that he was going on a date and didn't have time for this. He was not about to discuss his social life with the porter. Moreover, Andre was too agitated to pay attention.

A plastic yellow A-frame "CAUTION: WET FLOOR" sign guarded the compactor room door. Inside stood Calvin Birmingham and the police officer, who apparently had regained his composure.

"Calvin," Michael began, "what—"

Michael followed the trajectory of the superintendent's gaze to the white trash bags. He found himself in one last staring contest with Herman Matterweil, his opponent so many times at co-op board meetings.

"Oh, no," said Michael.

"Mr. Levine," said the porter, "You must help me."

Michael dimly heard Andre's voice, but felt tied to Herman's eyes.

That thing – that head – looked just like Herman, but Michael (and he hated himself for even thinking this) had never seen Herman looking so detached.

"Oh, no," repeated Michael. "Poor Herman. When did this happen?"

"You are my only hope," said Andre. "You must help me."

"Sure," said Michael absently. "When did this happen?"

"I don't know," said Birmingham. "Castellano just found him"

"People here will think I did that terrible thing to Mr. Matterweil," said Andre.

"You got that right," said Birmingham.

"Oh" said Michael, "I don't—"

"They will. I can feel it. I have watched enough television to know it. I found it – them – him. That makes me suspect number one. It happens all the time."

"Well—"

"You, Mr. Levine, must clear my name."

"I don't see a real problem here for you."

"These people will think I killed poor Mr. Matterweil," said Andre. "For me that is a problem. My goose is cooked. My name is mud. Unless you help me."

"Andre."

"Promise me, you'll clear my name."

"I—"

"Promise me."

This is foolish, thought Michael. But the man is scared. He just needs to know that somebody is in his corner. As pledges go this is easy to keep.

"Sure," said Michael.

"You have just made a solemn promise," intoned Andre.

Solemn promise, thought Michael. Whoa! I'd better check the fine print on this one. Herman was good at checking fine print. Oh, poor Herman. He was such a bastard; but this is no way to go. Why can't I remember something good about him?

Michael, ready to embark on his adventure with the unknown but no doubt fabulous Dolores Caruso, returned to his apartment to finish preparing for his date.

Perhaps I should cancel, thought Michael. Nah, it's too complicated to explain. And besides after what I've been through, I need this date. My first date in months — and now this happens to me.

Didn't happen to me, he corrected himself. It happened to Herman. Even now, he's making trouble for me. Why can't I think of something good about Herman? I'm probably just acknowledging that Herman wasn't a friend and I'm not in mourning and a date is not inappropriate behavior.

As Moscowitz eased into the Eastern Parkway service road that led to Olmsted Court, he saw the whirling lights of patrol cars, and double-parked television news vans.

You don't have to run away to join the circus, he thought. Just stay with the Department.

TWO

Yes Indeed

Michael Levine stood in the doorway of a SoHo loft building, far away from Olmsted Court. A homeless man furiously poked through a trash bin, and pulled out three empty Shasta soda cans. Michael stiffened. He half-expected to see one of Herman Matterweil's limbs plucked and held aloft.

I should talk to him, thought Michael. I should learn his story. I should become a restless advocate for this poor homeless man until he has regained his place in society. I should give him therapy; although I sense he's not ready for it. I should at least give him a quarter; but I just don't have any change.

The homeless man raised his head and stared at Michael's face. Michael stood still and waited for the scrutiny to end. The man spat on the pavement, and moved toward the next bonanza of empty cans.

Upstairs, Dolores Caruso, a woman Michael never had met, awaited him. Michael liked the concept of being awaited. This was his first date since he and Ellen Goldstein broke up 10 weeks earlier.

This evening had been sponsored by the Meachams, friends ever since Brooklyn College days. The Meachams told Michael about Dolores Caruso's blonde hair and fine sense of humor. They added, "She's a photographer and has been preparing for an exhibition."

"What did you tell her about me?" asked Michael.

"Oh, not too much," said Billy Meachams. "We said you weren't as bad as you seemed." Billy smiled.

Ha...ha, thought Michael. Why do so many people like to make fun of me? At least, Billy said I was better than I seemed. That's some kind of a compliment. Isn't it?

Michael rang the doorbell, and waited for an answering buzzer or a light to brighten the sliver of air beneath the door. Instead, a window on the third floor clattered open. A head, distinguished by long sandy blonde hair, poked out.

"Yes?"

"I'm Michael Levine."

"Be right down," she said, and slammed the window.

Four minutes later, Michael gasped as Dolores walked through the door and onto the street. Long, curly blonde hair, a glowing aura, framed her face. Her blue eyes suggested intelligence and a sense of play. Her simple white dress diagrammed her small, round breasts; exaggerated hips; and muscular thighs. A royal purple handknit shawl about her shoulders and large spherical rhinestone earrings completed the picture.

"Hi, Chester," said Dolores.

Michael was about to correct her when he heard a voice behind him exclaim, "Hiya honey."

9

It was the homeless man.

"Shall we go?" Dolores asked Michael.

"Yes," said Michael. "Yes, indeed."

And that's when Dolores saw his eyes. She was thankful for his neat attire— tweed jacket, dark brown slacks, subdued blue dress shirt and blue and red rep tie. But his eyes looked to her as if he understood the pain of others.

As they moved on, Michael wanted to tell Dolores about what happened in his building; but he didn't know how to work murder into a conversation without looking a little strange.

Instead he asked, "How did you know that guy's name?"

"We live in the same neighborhood," she replied. "He's an artist, although he is a bit crazy. He's shown me some of his drawings. Weird, fabulous stuff."

"He spit at me," said Michael, "but you know his name and all about his life.

"Oh," said Dolores, "I talk with him."

Time seemed to be on skates. They walked through Chinatown, and Michael winced every time he passed roast ducks hanging in the windows.

Dead ducks, he thought. Murdered ducks.

At Wong Kee's, Michael ordered steamed vegetables, and recoiled when Dolores proffered a taste of her ribs. He recounted the steps that led to his being a psychotherapist.

Somewhere during their stroll to the Cinema Village, Dolores nonchalantly put her arm through Michael's. As she did so, her hair brushed his neck and he enjoyed the sudden intense inhalation of her perfume. He thought of Ellen, and Ellen's aroma.

Can I miss Ellen, he wondered, and still like being with Dolores? Can I be having such a good time after what happened to Herman?

The theater's double bill of *Face in the Crowd* and *The Great Man* had the proper blend of melodrama and depth. Actually, Michael misunderstood the theater's schedule and thought they were going to see *Last Tango In Paris* and *In the Realm of the Senses*.

In The Cupping Room, a SoHo coffee house, Dolores discussed the eight months she spent photographing Ozark folk artists.

"The people were so wonderful," said Dolores. "These crafts-people are like Mozart and Haydn. They have a certain way of making things, a certain form they follow. Each piece is made like the other. The variations are subtle. And that's what makes each piece so special. I particularly remember Billy MacDonald, the chairmaker. He has a way of pulling your leg. I had just been down there a few days, and I still had my New York photojournalist clothes on.

"'Tell me,' I said, 'why do you do this?'"

"'I must be feebleminded,' Billy said. 'I beg your pardon?' I asked.

"'Well,' he said, 'you never know when you make these things if they're going to turn out exactly right. There's no instant gratification. So you've got to be feebleminded if you're going to make chairs with any degree of commitment.'"

As Michael laughed at her story, he turned his head away and then back. She was looking at him, and smiling. He felt so warm and lucky. God bless the Meachams, he thought.

11

THREE

Ulterior Motive

Dolores and Michael walked back to her loft building, Michael wondered why the Gods were willing to be so kind to him. There was this fabulous woman person creature right next to him. He also was amazed at how well he was handling his exposure to Herman's misfortune. There was no guilt. And why should there be? It was sad, but he and Herman had never been friends.

No Narcissus here, thought Michael. I am not making Herman's death something that happened to me.

At the building, Dolores searched for and found her keys. She turned her back to him as she opened the door.

"Dolores," he said softly.

She turned to him.

Those eyes, he thought. I could swim in those eyes.

He reached forward and took her hands. She moved closer to him. His arms went behind her, and brought her tightly to him. Gently, he kissed her cheek, and then moved his mouth to hers. They stayed that way for a comfortable while. Finally, they eased apart.

Michael followed Dolores into the elevator.

Whoa, she thought. Not tonight. My exhibit.

"I had a good time, Michael," said Dolores, "but I have a lot of work to do tomorrow for my exhibit and I'm very tired now."

"I had an ulterior motive," he said. "I have to use a bathroom."

"Okay," she said, "but I really don't have time for anything else."

As he stood in the bathroom, Michael could hear Dolores moving about her home. Though he could not see her, he just knew that every step, every swing of her arm was incredibly graceful.

How can I leave now, he thought, when things are going so well?

Dolores heard the sudden rush of water swirling through the commode.

Okay, she thought, we'll kiss once more. Maybe twice. Maybe three times. We'll say goodnight and then I can make my to-do list for tomorrow.

In the kitchen, Michael noticed a half-filled bottle of Beaujolais, which he retrieved along with two crystal glasses. He poured the wine. Dolores walked into the kitchen and observed the Beaujolais tableau.

"Oh crap," she said. "I don't have time for this."

"Come on," said Michael.

As Michael said this, he stretched his arm out imploringly. His hand collided with a wine goblet. Michael and Dolores both looked on in horror as the crystal slowly whirled on its base, gave up, fell over, hit the floor and shattered – but not before lackadaisically tossing its contents over the table's edge and on to Dolores's dress. A crimson stain methodically spread across the white dress.

"Blood," Michael whispered.

"I don't believe this," Dolores muttered. "Would you please leave?"

"I just wanted to—"

"I still see you."

"But, I didn't mean—"

"Please go."

"I'm not really this bad."

Dolores walked to the door. Michael followed and then paused.

Perhaps this would be a good time to tell her about Herman. Probably not.

"Do you suppose," he asked, "I might see you again?"

"Go!"

As Michael walked onto the street, he thought he heard Dolores laughing.

I'm ruined, he thought. Why was I so stupid? He thought about when he asked his psychopathology professor why bipolars didn't take their medication.

"It's their goddamn nature," the professor cackled.

Add me, Michael thought, to the list of people who can't help themselves.

By the time he returned home, only one vehicle, a blue-and-white, remained. New York City was just learning about Herman Matterweil and its collective nostrils quivered at the first whiff of the murder.

"This just in," declared the anchorman on the CBS 11:00 News. "A brutal slaying has taken place in the Park Slope section of Brooklyn. The victim, discovered by a building worker, was dismembered. Police are withholding the identity of the victim until next-of-kin can be identified."

Olmsted Courters who saw the broadcast and knew about the murder noted two oddities in the brief report. The anchorman got the neighborhood wrong. Olmsted Court was in Prospect Heights, not Park Slope. Also, it was the first time they ever had heard Herman Matterweil referred to as a victim.

Preoccupied with his own sore feelings, Michael walked briskly into the building and across the lobby to the elevator. As his key unlocked his door, Michael smiled for the first time. He was home, and for some stupid reason he felt safe.

FOUR

The Newsletter

While parts of the city slept and other parts gasped at Herman's murder, Blanche Copra labored in her kitchen. Seated at her maple table, she pulled her canary yellow number 2 pencil across her ever-present legal pad. Her close-cropped, gray hair, echoing her 55 years, resembled a hood. She occasionally paused to readjust her short frame into the chair, sedately shimmying in the process. Blanche was writing a rush edition of the building newsletter. Some material had been around; but the hot story that had to be circulated quickly was about poor Herman.

As she wrote, she remembered how she had grabbed control of the newsletter six months after Olmsted Court had been declared a co-op. The first editor was Louis Irving, a high school teacher. Irving only managed to create one issue.

"No," screamed Blanche when she read Louis Irving's newsletter. "What is this nonsense? What do you mean by this crap that Olmsted Court's new life as a housing cooperative is part of the global struggle for peace, freedom and justice?"

Louis smiled at her and said, "Well, isn't it?"

Blanche, in full fury, then called a special Board meeting.

"This is pie-in-the-sky garbage," she announced. "There's nothing here that tells the shareholders what they can and cannot do. No wonder people here are getting away with murder."

As she sat in her kitchen and grappled with Herman's obituary, she paused in observance. Oh, poor, dead Herman. People still were getting away with murder.

Blanche nearly kissed Herman when he put her in charge of the newsletter.

"You and I know this is a crusade," she told him. "We've got lots of riffraff living here, and we've got to root them out. We've got to prevent them from ruining our investment."

"I'm counting on you," Herman told her.

"There should also be information about nice things that are happening to some people," said Ethel Owens at that meeting.

"Sure," said Blanche offhandedly.

Blanche wondered what would have happened if she actually had kissed Herman. Would that have been the start of a fling? She knew she had caught Herman looking at her in that way. What would it have been like? Wouldn't they have had fun running the building together? Blanche shivered. This was not the right way to mourn someone who had been so thoroughly murdered. But in his own stuffy way, Herman Matterweil was quite the dreamboat. True, she thought, he was not a...well, he was not a pleasant man; but there was something about the way he could take charge and get what he wanted that just gave her goose bumps. If he had wanted her, she realized, she would not have been able to stop him.

Her newsletter chores usually gave Blanche a Cromwellian rapture. Occasionally, she felt stymied. Once, at Michael Levine's initiative, she was prevented from publishing the names of people who were behind in their monthly maintenance payments.

Michael and Blanche often voted against each other at Board meetings. Michael did not mind a difference of opinion. What he objected to, he explained reasonably, was "the crummy, bastardly methods she employed to obtain her slimy desires." In his calmer moments Michael felt that Blanche, like every human being, had a weird, fizzing, little chemistry set in her head. He envisioned chemistry sets walking around, bumping into each other, spilling on each other, blowing up. No wonder, he thought, life is such a puzzle.

Blanche typed six copies of the newsletter draft, containing the Herman Matterweil murder story. At approximately 7:00 a.m., she slipped these under the doors of Boardmembers.

At 8:30, cup of coffee in hand, Michael walked from his kitchen to his living room. Three folded 8 1/2 x 11 pieces of paper interrupted his path. He bent over and picked them up.

TO: BOARD OF DIRECTORS

SUBJECT: MATERIAL SCHEDULED FOR NEXT NEWSLETTER

The next Newsletter is being prepared, and all Board members are obliged to read, review and give comment. If

I hear nothing by this Monday, the newsletter will be printed and distributed.

Blanche Copra

This newsletter offered the usual Blanche compulsions: Old-Testament denunciations of those not paying monthly maintenance on time; and complaints about unleashed dogs and uncaring bicycle riders, all of which made havoc in the lobby. Then, of course, there was the big one.

Michael raised his coffee cup to his lips and reread the last paragraphs.

> The remains of Herman Matterweil were pulled out of the trash compactor. It is an awful, shocking crime and we will miss our noble leader. The Board wishes to extend condolences and all good wishes to the relatives of Herman Matterweil, in behalf of all Olmsted Courters.

Michael felt Blanche treated Herman's death as some little afterthought to the newsletter. How cavalier. Michael groped for the phone and dialed.

"Blanche, about this newsletter—"

"Oh, hello Michael."

"The Newsletter."

"I think it had a really special tone this time. Don't you?"

"Blanche I don't know that using the newsletter is the best way to get this news out to the shareholders."

"Ahh," sneered Blanche, "some more of Michael's precious sanctimony. You hated Herman's guts. Everybody knows that. And now you have the nerve to say we're treating him coldly."

Michael tightened his grasp of the phone, and marveled at how white his fingers became.

"I didn't hate Herman."

"It's a good thing they got that filthy little porter or the police would surely want to question you."

"They arrested Andre?"

"They didn't arrest him yet; but they did question him."

"That's absurd. He's a gentle guy."

"You were on Herman's mind before we lost him, Michael."

"Oh really?"

"Yes," said Blanche. "He felt that your psychotherapy practice brings too many crazy people into our lobby. He said it was bad for the building's security, and he wanted it stopped. I must say that I agree."

"Thank you for sharing."

After Michael hung up, he tried to sort out his feelings.

Is this how I'm supposed to remember Herman? The know-nothing who wanted to make life hard for my patients and me? I didn't hate Herman. I didn't. So why can't I conjure one good thought about him. It's not my fault that Herman had no sense of fun or fairness. For some of us, Olmsted Court no longer feels like home. I've seen people moved to rage by Herman. I can understand the source of murderous impulses; but it is wrong to tolerate antisocial behavior.

And then it all hit home.

Somebody that I probably know, thought Michael, violently murdered that poor, arrogant son-of-a-bitch. I wonder how the killer feels about me.

At the police station, Sergeant Bernard Moscowitz sat at the head of the table in an interrogation room. To his right was the two-page typed transcript of the questioning of Andre Castellano. There was nothing there. Moscowitz looked at the officers assigned to the Matterweil case.

I hate these briefing sessions, he thought. I hate it when cops act like they're in high school. They don't look at me, because they're afraid they're going to get called on.

"To summarize," said Moscowitz, "we know that Herman Matterweil was a run-of-the-mill autocrat, and is now very, very dead. He ran roughshod over everybody. His killer could have been someone from business, a spurned lover..."

"Maybe a lover who wishes she was spurned," offered one of the policemen.

The others laughed.

"Thank you Tatum," said Moscowitz. "That could be. Maybe a neighbor. This co-op stuff can be something fierce. Speaking of which, Tatum, talk to the building manager. All of these co-ops have outside managers to run their affairs. Maybe the killer is an avenging angel sent by God, or some other kind of Looney Tunes character. A careful application of Police Procedures 101 will yield answers that will lead us to the bad guy."

"There is no manager," said Tatum.

"What?"

"I already checked. There is no manager."

"Why make things easy for us," muttered Moscowitz.

"One warning," the sergeant continued, and his voice grew deadly soft. The other faces in the room cracked into attention.

"We," said Moscowitz, "are in a desert. Clues are like water in a desert. Once found, they must not be squandered, or spilled into the sand. For reasons that have nothing to do with public safety or justice, this is a high profile case. The media is all over us. Information cannot be given to the press without my permission. Bad guys read the papers and watch TV. It's not fair; but that's the way it is. We don't want them to know what we know until we want them to know it. That is policy."

Moscowitz stood and the meeting was over.

Back in Olmsted Court, the killer gazed through a living room window and liked the way the sun bounced off the police car windshield. It was going to be a bright, cheerful Saturday morning in May. In the Brooklyn Botanic Garden, across the street from Olmsted Court, the cherry trees were shedding their blossoms like so many snow flurries. Like the newspaper horoscope said, it was a good day to do your chores; not that anybody believed those things.

FIVE

Pampered Beauty

Monday morning was so saturated with spring that, for one perfumed moment at awakening, Michael recalled nothing of the previous night's events. And then the whole scenario crashed in. As morning proceeded, Michael repeatedly winced at the constant replay in his mind of Herman's face and the crimson wine slowly spreading on Dolores Caruso's dress.

"I'll just talk to her," he told himself. "I'll explain about Herman and confess what a total and complete jerk I am, and that I'm sorry. I'm sure she'll understand."

Michael enjoyed talking to himself. He had discovered the pleasure two months earlier when Ellen Goldstein, his girl friend of 18 months, left him.

Michael's intercom buzzed.

He glanced at his wristwatch.

Marjorie, he thought. I don't know if I'm ready for this.

"Your 10:00 nutcase is here," said Archie the doorman, calling from the lobby. "Do you really want me to send her up?"

Michael pursed his lips.

"He's thinking it over," Archie told the visitor.

"Her name is Ms. Gates," said Michael. "Please send her up. Oh — and Archie, I don't want my visitors insulted. Do it again, and I have no choice but to report you."

"Okay," said Archie, "but she has some mouth on her, Mr. Levine. You ought to tell her to behave herself."

Michael slowly returned the receiver to its cradle.

Archie was right. She did have a mouth on her. No passive aggressive, she.

This point was soon punctuated by Marjorie's thud-thud-thud assault on Michael's front door.

"That doorman of yours," said Marjorie Gates, as she strode into Michael's apartment. "Why don't you people fire him?"

"Well," said Michael, "firing would be—"

"This building is a co-op. Right?"

"Yes," said Michael, "but—"

"And you're on the board of this stupid co-op. Right?"

"I happen to be a boardmember, yes but—"

"Then, fire the bastard! Fire him for cause."

"I'll think about it," said Michael.

Marjorie Gates smiled and followed Michael into his office, which was once the apartment's dining room. She sat on the black leatherette chair next to his desk. She reached for an oval glass ashtray on the desk and slapped it down next to the box of Kleenex tissues. Michael placed a yellow legal pad on the center of his desk and, with a black Pentel pen, inscribed his patient's name and the date on the top line of the pad.

"How have you been this week?" asked Michael.

Marjorie reached for a Kleenex and squirmed in her seat. Once again, Michael noticed that Marjorie's heavy make-up and chubby cheeks lent her a certain pampered beauty. She wore a crimson vest over an ivory blouse, tucked into ebony culottes. Her feet rested in aquamarine flats.

Pampered beauty, thought Michael. That date came just in time.

"That doorman is always nasty to me," said Marjorie. "Although he's kind of cute. Do you think he was coming on to me?"

"Cute?" asked Michael. "No, I don't think he was coming on to you."

"Why not? I guess you don't think it possible that men find me attractive.

"On the other hand," continued Marjorie. "I couldn't care less about your opinion. If I had any brains, I'd see a real psychiatrist instead of some schmuck with a Master's."

You bitch, thought Michael, you're lucky that I'm willing to help you.

"Tell me more," he said.

"I'm surprised you're even seeing me today."

"And why is that?"

"The murder, stupid. How could you even go on as if nothing happened when someone you know, someone you worked with, was cut into little pieces and tossed in the trash? Don't you have any feelings?"

"Of course I do," he said, detecting a bit too much defensiveness in his response. "It's just that he and I were not what you would call friends. It's true that we did work together, and certainly I feel saddened."

Michael paused. He noticed that he felt not a shred of sadness and thought it quite interesting.

"A profound sadness," he continued, "but life goes on, and I feel a certain obligation to help the living. And that includes you."

Downstairs, in the Olmsted Court lobby Blanche Copra supervised Calvin Birmingham who was hanging a wreath, in honor of Matterweil, near the mailboxes.

Birmingham, a tall black man with high cheekbones, wore a sharply pressed light blue work shirt and work pants.

"Move it more to the left," she said. "Don't you know where your left is?"

"Yes, Miss Copra."

"That's better."

"Thank you, Miss Copra."

"That wreath gives a nice touch."

"Will we be doing any repairs before a new president is picked?"

"How can you even think of repairs at such a time?"

"Some people have problems, and Mr. Matterweil was going to help them."

"Like who? Like what?"

"Plastering in 8E."

"What kind of plastering?"

"To patch up the hole in the wall caused by the riser repair," said Birmingham.

"Those people are nincompoops. They don't deserve special service."

"Albert was supposed to do the job," said Birmingham.

"Albert?"

"Our part-time contractor."

26

"Oh, right, your brother -in-law. Tell your brother-in-law he could have the day off."

"He'd rather work," said Birmingham. "And besides, these people need the work done."

"He can work somewhere else," said Copra. "We have had a death in the family."

"I was eating a peanut butter and jelly sandwich," Marjorie told Michael. "I wanted to share it with my Snoopy doll. When I pushed the sandwich against his face, I smeared the sticky stuff all over him. Mommy had to wash him immediately. He came apart in the washing machine. He just fell into little pieces of cloth and lint and stuffing, floating belly-up in the water.

"When Mommy saw it, she started to laugh. She always did have a good sense of humor. She wanted me to laugh too; but I couldn't. I started to cry. I couldn't stop, even though Mommy told me to. She hit me, and I wouldn't stop crying. I didn't mean to make her mad but I just couldn't help myself. She started shouting, 'It's your own damned fault. If you knew how to take care of your toys, this never would have happened.' She was right, of course."

Marjorie reached for a tissue and dabbed at her eyes.

"I must have told you about this, before," she said.

"You have," said Michael, "except this is the first time you told me about your crying and your mother being abusive to you."

"My mother never, never has been abusive to me. She loves me."

"You can love someone and still abuse that person," said Michael.

"Is that what you did with your girlfriend? Is that why she dumped you?"

Michael's eyes widened, and Marjorie smiled briefly.

"That really hurt," said Michael.

"So? So why should I be the only one who gets hurt here?"

"That's exactly what we're talking about," said Michael. Feeling inspired, he continued. "Your favorite doll gets destroyed. Your mother laughs; you cry; she hits you, and yells at you. Why?"

"I made her yell."

"In order to make someone yell," said Michael, "wouldn't you have to be able to control their emotions and thoughts and nervous systems and bodies? And you were a child. How could the eight-year-old Marjorie make her adult mother yell?"

"You are so stupid. It's easy to make people go crazy. You just have to know which buttons to push."

"Your mother acted the way she did because of what was going on in her head – not what was going on in your head. You tried to adjust to her behavior. You were a kid. You didn't understand that she was having emotional problems of her own.

"But here's the thing Marjorie. When a person adapts too well to emotionally unhealthy behavior, that person puts her own emotional health at risk. Her own perceptions become skewed, and her own reactions inappropriate."

"You're talking about me."

"Well let's—"

"You're talking about me, and you're saying I'm crazy and my mother is crazy."

"We're talking about emotional health," said Michael, "and we're talking about what happens when you adapt to your mother's perceptions of herself, the world and you. Let's look at how you feel about this."

"No! Let's look at how you feel about it. This is how you get your kicks. You don't do anything. The closest you get to life is listening to other people's stories.

"My mother does love me, and any punishment I got was my fault. I made my mother yell at me. I make men mad at me, and right now I'm letting you belittle me. I should learn to protect myself, and I'll start right now. This session is over."

Marjorie abruptly arose, and rushed out of Michael's office. He stood but did not follow. The door quickly slammed and Michael returned to his desk and began to write his notes on the legal pad.

"MG seemed deeply troubled by the therapist's comments about her mother," Michael wrote. "Rather than explore the possibility that she was the target of an abusive parent, and the consequences of being raised in a dysfunctional environment, MG arbitrarily ended the session. In past sessions, she would dismiss such observations with ridicule or personal attacks against the therapist. The fact that she could not employ the familiar defenses deserves further study."

"I think we've just witnessed a breakthrough," Michael said aloud. "Of course Marjorie thinks that she inflicted damage by walking out on me just like Ellen did. I guess the joke's on her."

In the lobby Blanche Copra glanced at Marjorie Gates as she stomped across the polished floors. She watched Michael's patient pause beneath the canopy, light a cigarette and walk onto Eastern Parkway.

"That woman," Copra asked Archie, "does she live here? I've never seen her before."

"No," said Archie, "she doesn't live here. She's a nutcase. She's one of Levine's patients. What a mouth she's got."

"I don't like the idea of Levine letting crazy people in our building," said Copra. "Herman was right. We should have a rule against it."

SIX

Better Manners

Dolores Caruso was slicing vegetables when Juliet Meacham called.

"I'm in a rush," said Juliet, "so let's get straight to the dirt."

"And how are you?" asked Dolores.

"I'm fine. Don't I sound fine?"

"I don't know," said Dolores. "You sound like you might be coming down with a cold."

"Well, I do have a slight sniffle; but let's not talk about me. What's the story with Michael?"

"There's no story."

"Whoops. You didn't hit it off?"

"Let me ask you a question."

"Sure," said Juliet.

"You've seen me in a whole bunch of social situations. When I'm with guys, do I come on too much?"

"You've never turned me on."

"I'm serious," said Dolores.

"Oh, I don't know," said Juliet. "It's been years since I've been on a date. I don't really know what the rules are."

"We had dinner, movies, coffee," said Dolores. "We talked. I was having a great time. It seemed like he was too. Then he brought me back to the loft."

"So far, so good."

"I had a good time and I wanted to see him again."

"So?"

"This nice guy I spent a few hours with turned into Tarzan of the Apes."

"So?"

"I said good night to him as gently and firmly as possible. I explained that it had to be an early night because of this damned exhibit."

"So?"

"He lied to get inside the loft. And then he wanted to get romantic."

"I thought you could use a little romance."

"That's not the point," said Dolores. "I don't think I gave him any reason to believe I wanted him to stay."

"He didn't—"

"No, I got rid of him."

"So, what's the problem? He got a little carried away. That's a tribute to your charms. Was it hard to get him to leave?"

"No," said Dolores, "I guess it wasn't all that difficult to send him away. Although in the process, he did break one of those nice crystal goblets you gave me."

"That bastard!"

"The thing is," said Dolores, "this isn't the first time I've had a scene like this. I tell you, Afghani fighters have better manners than these New York men."

"So, it's deep six for Michael?"

"He didn't earn too many bonus miles," said Dolores.

"As I recall, you were the one who complained to me about your empty social life."

"I did mention something in passing," said Dolores. "You put your matchmaker hat on immediately, and I didn't have a chance to say anything."

"You could have said no."

"You guys built him up so much."

"Poor Dolores Caruso," said Juliet," just a reed in the wind."

Dolores smiled.

"You made him sound like a nice guy," said Dolores, "and I can use one of those in my life. I'll even grant you he's a cute guy. But what's the use of starting with someone if you know where the relationship is going to go?"

"Yeah," said Juliet, tragically, "why bother? Better to take up needlepoint."

Dolores laughed

"So," Juliet continued, "I have to tell William that the match-up failed?"

"No," said Dolores, "I'll probably go out with Michael again. What the hell."

"So I can report to William that the match-up was a success?"

"I'd call that an exaggeration," said Dolores. "You can tell him that we survived and that Michael and I might go out again. Only don't tell William yet because Michael doesn't know."

"So you think you and Michael might be an item?"

"Take it easy, Meacham. We had a date. We might have another date. Who knows? Other things happen to be going on in my life. I'm working on the most important

33

exhibition I've ever had. I think the pictures are really very special, and I get to show how my friends in the Ozarks live."

"Fine," said Juliet. "I've got to go."

"Me too," said Dolores, "I've got to get some Ilford paper."

When Dolores stepped outside, she saw Chester. He was sitting on the loading dock and delicately eating a slice of pizza.

"Hey Chester," she said, "How's it going."

"Okay, I guess," he said, "but I wish somebody would talk to the Pope. Now he wants me to do the ceiling in pink. Last month it was navy blue, and before that he wanted the ceiling in off-white."

"You know how patrons are," she said.

"I suppose you're right," said Chester. "Hey, is that guy who was here the other night coming back?"

"I don't know. Why?"

"I think he wanted to give me money; but he didn't know how?"

"So what do you think?" asked Dolores.

"I'm sorry to say it, honey; but I think he's a jerk – albeit a nice jerk."

"You could be right, Chester."

SEVEN

Not Herman

Sergeant Moscowitz stood in the corridor of Olmsted Court's sixth floor and consulted his notes. Some investigators treated canvassing as a sales call. They persuaded, cajoled, used every angle to build rapport and squeeze information from the subjects. Moscowitz treated the process as a ritual, a solemn occasion. He was the high priest and the subjects – dry-mouthed and humble – were inductees. He wore his "just the facts, ma'am" outfit — a tan suit, yellow dress shirt and dark brown silk tie. His cordovan wingtip shoes glowed with polish.

He already had checked off 12 names on his door-to-door list, and he didn't like what he was learning – namely, next to nothing.

Everybody had opinions about Matterweil. He was fair. He was mean. He was kind. He was rotten. But they knew nothing about the man.

"If you want to know the killer," Moscowitz liked to say," you've got to know the victim."

Moscowitz ran his finger down the list of residents. The next candidate for waste of time was Michael Levine, apartment 6D. He had gathered some juicy negatives about Levine; but nothing really incriminating. The detective stepped over to Levine's apartment and rang the bell.

"Good afternoon," said the detective. "I'm Sergeant Bernard Moscowitz, and I would like to ask you a few questions regarding the death of Herman Matterweil."

In the living room Moscowitz settled into a flowered wingback easy chair which Michael had purchased from a thrift shop on Flatbush Avenue. It was Michael's favorite chair. Michael immediately sat down on the steel gray couch.

"Did you say," asked Michael, "that your name is Moscowitz?"

"That's right."

People always had to question Moscowitz about his name, as if it really were their business. He was used to people being rude; but he found it incredibly boring to have to tell strangers that his black Baptist mother and his white Jewish father fell in love and got married. Sometimes he modified the story.

"I changed my name," he told Michael.

"Oh really?"

"I didn't want to have a slave name, anymore."

"Oh," said Michael.

The policeman removed a small, black loose-leaf notebook from his right-hand jacket pocket, and opened it to a blank page. He removed a stick ballpoint pen from his shirt pocket, uncapped the point, and suspended the pen over the blank page.

"Mr. Levine," Moscowitz began, "as I said, I am investigating the murder of Herman Matterweil. Your cooperation will be very helpful. I'm going to ask you a few questions. Answer them as completely as you can. A scrap of information that means nothing to you may be crucial to us. Do you understand?"

"Yes," said Michael.

"Good," said Moscowitz. "First, I'd like you to tell me what you know about Mr. Matterweil's murder."

"Not much," said Michael. "The porter found him and brought me downstairs, and I saw the bags."

"What can you tell me about Herman Matterweil?"

"Herman and I were not the best of friends," began Michael. "He never really confided in me. What I know about him I guess is the public story.

"He was a longtime tenant here, and I suppose he always interacted well. I never really noticed him – until the landlord decided to convert the building into a co-op. All of a sudden, Herman got religion. He wanted everybody in this building to buy in."

"Why was that?"

"He said we had invested so much of our lives in Olmsted Court; but the building wouldn't be truly ours until we invested money. He said we could control our destinies, actually own the building that was so much a part of us, and each have a tidy investment to boot.

"It was very important to him that we all buy in. He didn't want anybody to lose out. In the course of doing this, he had a number of clashes with tenants."

"Including you?"

Ouch, thought Michael.

"Yes, including me," he said. "But I really admired that sudden sense of community. He saw that the co-op was going to happen and was a good idea and he wanted this community to move intact into the next phase, and to derive the benefits. I'm a psychotherapist and from time to time I'm privileged to see some event transform a life. Clearly, that's what happened here."

"So, now that you all own Olmsted Court," asked Moscowitz, "how much money is involved?"

"I don't have the exact figures," Michael replied. "I do know there's over a million in annual income, and I think $150,000 in a reserve fund."

"And I understand there's no management company, helping you all with this," said Moscowitz.

"That's right," said Michael. "Herman said we didn't need one. He said there was enough talent in Olmsted Court to run the building's affairs quite well, and management fees were an unnecessary extravagance — at least for us. And he was right."

"Did Mr. Matterweil show any sudden signs of affluence— a new car, new clothes, new television set, vacations?"

"Not Herman," said Michael. "It seems to me he lived a very austere life, although he could afford better. He was a retired businessman, some kind of garment manufacturer."

"What about Mr. Matterweil's romantic life?"

"Not Herman. He was an old-time bachelor who tipped his hat to the ladies and played cards on Thursday nights."

"Did he seem to enjoy gambling?"

"Sergeant, Herman didn't seem to enjoy anything."

"Did Herman Matterweil have any enemies?" asked Moscowitz.

"I don't know. I can't imagine who would be so hostile as to — as to —"

"Murder him?"

"Yes."

"I've read," said Moscowitz, "that people in co-ops don't get along. Is that true here? Or did things settle down after you became a co-op?"

"We've had our little disagreements," said Michael. "Our occasional shouting matches. There have been a few lawsuits, and maybe a fistfight or two; but I don't think we've had any real trouble."

Moscowitz looked at his notebook, and turned to a spot three pages earlier.

"What can you tell me about Castellano, the porter?"

"Like what?" Michael asked.

"Like anything. Habits? Temperament? Did he and Matterweil have any problems with each other?"

"Certainly not," said Michael, seeing an opportunity to keep his solemn promise.

"Not even when Matterweil threatened to pull Castellano off the night shift?"

"Andre was more confused and hurt than angry. He only shouted at Herman because of all the frustration he felt."

Michael saw Moscowitz write something in the notebook.

I'm doing a real great job of clearing Andre's name, thought Michael.

"Andre has another job, and he was just afraid he'd have to quit one of the places," explained Michael. "He didn't really threaten Herman. He just tried to curse him out; but he couldn't think of any really good swear words."

Moscowitz added a new note, and then leafed forward to a clean page.

"Mr. Levine. If I understand correctly, you and Mr. Matterweil did not get along."

"I had real difficulty with his arrogance," said Michael. "It was do it his way or else, and sometimes that made him an unpleasant person to deal with."

"I understand," said Sergeant Moscowitz, "that on one occasion you called Mr. Matterweil a 'stupid, bloated fascist?'"

"I might have."

"And you also said that his existence was a blotch on God's record."

Moscowitz stared at Michael and noticed the psychotherapist flinch ever so slightly. It seemed to the policeman that in every interrogation, questioning, or taking of a statement there was a special moment. It was the moment when the subject realized he or she was staring real life right in the face. The Sergeant liked to think of himself as real life incarnate.

"Sergeant Moscowitz, am I a suspect?"

There was no response, and Michael turned his gaze to the window.

He saw two pigeons suddenly rising. He pressed his lips together, and leaned back on the couch. He even folded his hands.

"Did you," Moscowitz asked, "make that statement?"

"I think I said something to that effect; but there was a reason."

"Of course. Where were you late Friday afternoon, Mr. Levine?"

"I was right here, by myself, getting ready for a date."

"It takes you all afternoon to prepare for an evening out?"

"It's been awhile since I've dated. I'm out of practice."

Michael smiled, but Moscowitz did not return the smile.

"And then," continued Moscowitz, "after seeing the victim's remains, you went out on a date?"

"Maybe it was the wrong thing to do; but I was looking forward to it – the date – for a long time. It was the wrong thing to do."

Moscowitz looked at his notebook.

I am indeed a suspect, thought Michael.

Michael recounted the whole evening, and even told Moscowitz about the spilled wine.

"Actually," said Michael, "despite the embarrassment; I'm glad I had a chance to talk about it and get it off my chest."

Moscowitz smiled.

"That," he said, "is one way we get killers to confess."

Now I've gone and done it, Michael thought.

"Sometimes," said Moscowitz, "we interrogate people who have committed pretty heinous crimes."

Moscowitz smoothly arose, and glided to a point, just behind the couch, where Michael sat.

"We say to them," said Moscowitz softly, "here's your chance to tell us what happened. You'll feel so much better when you do."

"And do they?"

Oh God, thought Michael, I'm sure I sound like a perpetrator.

"Sometimes they do," said Moscowitz.

This guy's no killer, thought Moscowitz.

"I'm sure you've said that to a patient at some time."

"No, not really."

"You might try it. You can save them a lot of money and yourself a lot of boredom."

"My clients want to talk to me. I think your clients hire lawyers to do that for them."

"That may be, but I'll bet you can get a lot of juicier material from them if you try it. You might even learn something that I'd love to know."

"Like what?"

"I think I have all the information I need right now, Mr. Levine," said Moscowitz, as he walked to the front door. "May I contact you if I need anything else?"

"Sure," said Michael.

After the door closed behind the Sergeant, Michael sat very still as if an unwanted visitor was knocking on his door.

EIGHT

Poor, Poor Man

This is ridiculous, Michael thought. I didn't kill Herman. Nevertheless, he could almost hear the solid clang of a closing jail cell. He didn't want to spend his last hours of freedom listening to someone else's problems. He called Aaron Bitofsky, his only other appointment for the day.

"Aaron," Michael said, "we have to cancel this afternoon's session."

"Oh," said Aaron. "Did I do something wrong last time?"

"No, you were very helpful. There was a little accident in my building Friday night, and—"

"Oh, you live in that building where that poor, poor man was cut up into little pieces and tossed into the garbage."

"Something like that; but—"

"And," said Aaron, "you call that a little accident? Now I guess the cops want to talk to you? Did you do it?"

"No, of course not."

"Then why do they want to quiz you?"

"The investigator on this case already came to me for help. We already had a conversation."

"I knew it. So they gave you the third degree already, eh?"

"Aaron, I have a lot of things to do and so I have to run now," Michael said. "Let's reschedule."

He turned to his Week-at-a-Glance calendar, and found the blank pages.

"Let's make it this Thursday at the same time, 3:00. Is that okay with you?"

"Why do I have to come and go, according to your whims?"

"Is Thursday inconvenient?"

"No, of course not. It's just that I never get to set an appointment, and that makes me angry."

"Perhaps at our next session," said Michael, "we'll take up the issue of hostility."

"Fuck you," Aaron said, as he hung up.

Michael had little to do; but he was too disoriented to do it. Perhaps he needed the reassurance that comes from engaging in petty tasks. He would finish washing the coffee pot. No, he would take out the garbage and then go for a newspaper. The Key Foods shopping bag contained four days worth of coffee grounds, three empty Breyer's vanilla yogurt containers, two Tropicana orange juice quart cartons, a bag that once held Wise's potato chips, the remains of some chili he attempted to make, and 16 days worth of junk mail.

It also held the crumpled letter that he wrote to Ellen; but never mailed.

"I love you," he had written. "Please come back. I need you. I promise to always show you how much I care."

44

He couldn't bring himself to send that letter and he wasn't sure why. He knew that he either meant everything that he said or, at least, wanted to mean everything that he said.

Michael stepped out of his apartment with his trash, and pressed the elevator "down" button. In the compactor area, he opened the door that led to the shaft. It was very much like opening a mailbox on the street. He placed the shopping bag in the receptacle, closed the door and listened to the satisfying sounds of clattering food cartons and fluttering paper diving downward.

Michael thought of Herman's last journey, and muttered, "Rest in peace, you poor bastard." He wondered if he would think of Herman every time garbage had to be taken out.

As the descending elevator cab approached, Michael heard overtones of an animated conversation. The door opened and the cab's occupants, Evelyn Ross and Roberta Haven looked at Michael, looked at each other, and overtly, uncharacteristically curtailed their interchange.

"Hello, Michael," they chorused.

He nodded.

Both women were 60-years-old; but they had little in common. Evelyn Ross grew up on the Lower East Side a few miles away from and several social classes below Olmsted Court. Her alcoholic father and vitriolic mother taught Evelyn to scream for what she wanted. Mostly, she wanted more —and other. Her ticket out was an intern, Dr. Aaron Ross. They met in the Mother Cabrini Hospital Emergency Room where he removed a cinder from her right eye.

That was the next to last thing she gave him. From there on in, she knew that as a doctor's wife, it was her right to take. The Olmsted Court era Evelyn Ross was dark-haired, slim and equipped with large, expressive, watery eyes. Her heavy make-up, tintinnabulating bracelets, and designer fashions suggested her own guerrilla skirmishes with time and status.

Roberta Haven wore her gray hair in braids. Olmsted Courters knew that she was from Oklahoma, lived off a trust fund, and had a passion for gardening. She was often seen working on the fenced-in patch of soil that fronted the building. Raking, troweling, wheelbarrow pushing was her life. The exercise helped keep her body trim, and she had a fluidity of movement that Michael found attractive.

"Think it will rain?" asked Michael.

Roberta dabbed at her eye.

The elevator door opened and the three stepped onto the terrazzo lobby floor. Evelyn glided, Michael slumped and Roberta sobbed. Suddenly, Evelyn turned around and pointed her finger at Michael.

"And another thing," she said. "I have a terrible leak in the bathroom. I suppose you people will have to pick a new President before anything gets done."

"Do you think the new president will let me continue to work in the garden?" asked Roberta.

"I'm sure of it," said Michael. "After all, you're a tradition."

"It's very kind of you to say that, Mr. Levine; but I am given to understand that not everybody feels that way," said Roberta.

That was true. Some Olmsted Courters felt that a resident should not be seen doing the sort of manual labor that should be done by the staff. They felt it demeaned the building's image and would adversely affect apartment values.

As Evelyn Ross and Roberta Haven moved toward the front door, Archie assembled his loose body into a coiled spring and smartly opened the door. Most newcomers to Olmsted Court marveled at Archie's style.

"It's a swell day today, Mr. Levine," observed Archie, as Michael moved across the threshold. "Too bad about all those people who are refusing to pay their maintenance."

"What?"

"I heard that some people aren't going to pay maintenance until the killer is found."

"That's ridiculous!"

"That's what I thought; but you know how rumors work. Why worry about it? Like I said, it's a nice day today."

Michael chose to think about the weather. He saw that the sky was clear, the temperature fair, and he felt a companionable breeze. He headed for Oscar's newsstand around the corner.

A few copies of *Jet* were stuck into the magazine rack. Scattered about the counter were various items for sale — horse race tip sheets, handkerchiefs, batteries, incense, etc. The automatic coffee maker wafted the aroma of strong coffee into the air. Oscar, a tall, black, completely bald man, pulled a package of Salem menthol cigarettes from beneath the counter and extracted three cigarettes. Placing the three "loosies" on the counter, he said, "Here you go, Tanya."

"Thank you, baby," she said.

Michael eyed the newspapers resignedly. The *New York Post* headline declared, "CRAZED SLASHER

DEFIES COPS." The *Daily News* was more sedate. It merely trumpeted, "CO-OP KILLER STILL AT LARGE."

"Hey Michael, how are you doing?" said Oscar.

"Okay," replied Michael.

"Then you haven't read the papers yet."

"No, but I will."

"Be strong; have courage; keep the faith."

"Must I do all those things?" asked Michael.

"Two out of three and you'll be okay," said Oscar. "Two out of three, man."

Michael entered the Olmsted Court lobby as Sergeant Moscowitz was leaving. The two men nodded to each other.

Two out of three, thought Michael, and I'll be okay.

Michael sat on the winged-back chair in his living room, and opened the *News*. Page 3 featured a picture of Olmsted Court. An inset photograph of Herman Matterweil stared gravely outward from its cushion of words. It was contained within a sidebar article headlined "Neighbors Shocked."

Where, Michael wondered, did they get that picture? Did they take it from his apartment? Did a relative give it to them? How did they get it in time for this morning's paper? Did they always have it just in case?

Michael read the article.

Neighbors Shocked

Today, a question-mark hangs over Olmsted Court, a luxury co-op for the affluent in Brooklyn's gentrified Prospect Heights community. Who brutally slew Herman Matterweil Friday night and why?

Matterweil, 67, was the co-op board president, and by all accounts a respected leader of the community.

"He had a lot of dignity," said one Olmsted Court resident who did not wish to be identified. "He always was such a gentleman. I just can't believe it."

Dazed expressions are common in Olmsted Court these days. A trusted friend is gone. Also, there is the unspoken knowledge that violence has come in off the streets and knocked on one of their doors.

Doorman Herbert Calloway, affectionately referred to as Archie, has been with Olmsted Court for 27 years. He feels this might be its saddest moment.

"This is terrible, just terrible," said Calloway. "Mr. Matterweil was a good guy. People around here ask me who's going to be next."

The police may be asking the same question. Did Matterweil have an enemy? Did the murderer have a motive? Or is there a homicidal maniac on the loose in Olmsted Court?

Aha, thought Michael. A multiple choice question. Why do we always want each murder to be accompanied by a neat, comprehensible reason for said crime? We hear about a slaying and we must know the details. We must know if there were any justice or at least some law of natural determination that led to the event.

We want our murderers to be poor and exploited, or quiet and seething, or rich and spoiled. We want the killer to be a spurned lover, or a burglar caught in the act, or a hit man doling out judgment.

We want the victim to cross some invisible line. The victim should never have fallen in love with the murderer. The victim should not have tried to hold on to those last few dollars. The victim should not have insulted, embarrassed, or ridiculed the murderer. The victim should not have been a drug user or a model or a libertine or a bus driver. The victim should have moved from the neighborhood. The victim should have been somewhere else.

We want to feel that we never could have been the victim. We want to study all the minutiae of the murder. We want to be forensic passersby and reconstruct the one secret never possessed by the victim— How to avoid being murdered.

And yet, if everything in life is an education, then why not murder?

The phone rang.

"Hello," said Michael.

"Hi Michael, This is Walter."

"Hello, Walter. What's up?"

"Herman's funeral is tomorrow at 11 am," said Walter, "and there will be a Board meeting at 8:00 tomorrow night."

Michael grabbed the pen, resting on top of his refrigerator, and a pad of Postit notes.

"Where are the services?" he asked.

"Rohrberg Funeral Home on Coney Island Avenue. And Michael?"

"Yes?"

"We'd like you to say a few words at the services?"

"Me?"

"Yes!"

"Why me? Herman and I were not exactly what you'd call close," said Michael.

"Yes, I know," said Walter, "you couldn't stand each other."

"So what is this," asked Michael. "Some kind of a joke?"

"Somebody representing the Board should speak, and your name came up most often."

"Oh, really? That's very flattering."

"I'm glad you're taking it that way," said Walter.

"What other way could there be?" asked Michael.

"Oh, you know."

"No, I don't know."

"Well," said Walter with a people-are-funny chuckle, "some of our neighbors actually think there's a killer running loose through Olmsted Court."

"No kidding," said Michael, trying to echo Walter's chuckle.

"Right! And they think that whoever speaks at the funeral is a target."

"That's rich," said Michael. He paused. "So, when you were looking for the right speaker, my name kept coming up?"

"Right," said Walter. "Short straw, name being pulled from a hat, coin-flipping. Yours was the name that came up most often. Listen, I have a few more calls to make, so I'll see you tomorrow."

Michael heard the click at the other end.

NINE

It's Your Funeral

The morning of Herman's funeral brought rain to Olmsted Court.

"God is showing us His sorrow," Walter Warren said to Calvin Birmingham in the lobby. Birmingham nodded. It seemed the safest thing to do.

"At least God gets to go to the funeral," said Archie. "I've got to stay here and watch the door."

Michael looked at the steady drizzle through a lobby window and wondered how he'd get to the Funeral Home.

"Hey Levine," boomed a voice from behind. "You want a lift?"

"Sure," said Michael and spun around.

Even as he turned, he realized the voice belonged to Krane the salesman. Suddenly, Michael knew the taste of despair; but it was too late. Krane told jokes relentlessly, remorselessly, repeatedly. A few were funny; but all were in bad taste. And he knew so many of them. It wasn't just that he told jokes. It was absolutely essential that his audience laughed. If one story didn't work, maybe the next one would, or the next one or the next.

Even this would be okay if Krane then walked away in triumph. The first sign of laughter only encouraged him. He felt he had you, and that he was on a roll. Now, there would be no mercy. The jokes would continue.

But we're going to a funeral, thought Michael who really didn't want to travel by bus. Surely, even Krane understands that.

"I'm parked down the block," said Krane as he and Michael walked past Archie and into the street. They turned right on Eastern Parkway.

"A sad day for Olmsted Court," said Krane.

"Right," said Michael.

"It brings back memories of other funerals."

"True," said Michael.

"I'm thinking about my friend, Marlene," said Krane. "She died about a year ago."

"I'm sorry to hear about that," said Michael.

"Yeah," said Krane, "It was very sad. She was a streetwalker in Paris, and then she moved to Venice. Drowned to death, you know. Well, here's the car."

Michael managed a rueful smile as Krane unlocked the passenger side door of his red Oldsmobile Cutlass.

"Just toss that stuff into the back," said Krane, pointing to a briefcase and a shopping bag filled with maps.

Krane was silent as the car started to move. Could it be, thought Michael.

"Actually," said Krane, "Marlene's name used to be Virginia."

No, it couldn't be.

"Yeah," continued Krane, "when I met her I called her Virgin for short; but not for long.

"Here's a good one. There was this Israeli guy, and this Czechoslovakian guy, and they went walking in the woods..."

Many jokes later, the bright red Cutlass slid to a halt in front of the funeral parlor. Krane stayed behind the wheel. He had to finish his story. Michael dared not move.

"And so," said Krane, "the third suitor said, 'you two guys move over. You're sitting on my Billybob.' The young woman turned to her mother and said, 'That's the man I want to marry.'

"You know," said Krane in awe, "that joke came all the way from the Ozarks. I found it in a book."

The Ozarks, thought Michael. I wonder if Dolores heard that joke when she was taking pictures there. Who would dare tell it to her?

"I better get this car parked," said Krane. "So you can get out over here."

Upon entering the Rohrberg Funeral Home, Michael was rocked by a familiar sensation. He felt as if he were a child again and was visiting his Great Aunt Ruth. The furniture was overstuffed; he had to sit very, very still; he had to be very, very quiet; and there was nobody to play with.

He found a pile of yarmulkes near the door, and slipped one upon his head. The skull cap sent a sudden wave of solemnity through Michael's body. Self-consciously, he removed his hands from his jacket pockets. A black board with white plastic letters directed mourners to the various services.

Herman Matterweil — Room B.

Michael entered a room with light blue walls and thick brown carpeting. A faded, flowered couch hugged one wall. Beige, bulbous lamps with faintly oriental motifs, and square purple glass ashtrays stood on tables. Arm-chairs and straight-back dining room chairs waited against two other walls.

Amber spotlights dramatically displayed Herman's casket, located in front of the fourth wall. Roses, lilies, and other brightly-hued floral offerings surrounded the sealed, highly-polished mahogany coffin.

The room was filled with Olmsted Courters. As Michael walked toward the casket, he heard snippets of conversation.

"I think Herman only had another 10 pounds to go on his diet."

"I never knew any layman who understood the law as well as Matterweil did."

"We're thinking of buying some land in Maine."

"In our bathroom the toilet just keeps flushing..."

Andre Castellano sat on a straight-back chair. He wore a blue suit, white shirt and green tie.

"Andre," said Michael, "you're here."

"Thank you Mr. Levine," said Andre, "for making a big deal out of it. I am simply here to pay my respects to my employer, something an innocent person, which is what I am, can easily do."

"Well, of course, you're innocent," said Michael.

A few heads turned in their direction. Andre gestured for silence by rolling his eyes sharply.

"Thank you, Mr. Levine, for all your help."

"Sure," said Michael who turned away only to see an approaching Blanche Copra. She wore a navy blue dress, pearls, and a black cloth fur-trimmed hat with veil.

"Oh Michael, it's about time you're here. When I heard you were going to speak, I said, 'at last, we'll get some use out of him.'"

"Thank you for that ringing vote of confidence," said Michael.

"It just so happens," said Blanche, "that as annoying as you are, I want you to do well. You'll be representing the Board when you speak. If you don't care, however, I guess it's just your funeral."

"Actually, it's Herman's," said Michael

"Well, you know what I mean," she said, and flounced away.

Doors to the chapel swung open.

Michael looked at his wristwatch. 10:55. That would give the crowd just enough time to mill and be seated by 11:00 exactly. He imagined that there was an Old Man Rohrberg somewhere who would tell his sons over and over again, "Give the people what they want. People want funerals they can count on. Boom. Boom. In and out. They come in, pay their respects, have a decent service, and walk out of this place. They get what they want, and we get our rewards – higher turnover per day."

And the sons would say, "Yes papa; yes, papa."

A sparsely-bearded young man, wearing a three-piece pin-striped suit and a fedora, entered the chapel from a front side door and stepped slowly to the rostrum. Apparently, he was a rabbi. He opened his prayer book and removed a folded piece of lined notebook paper. His palms were extended outwards. As if measuring justice, he brought his hands slightly upwards. The mourners rose in a movement that resembled a baseball stadium wave.

"So that's the rabbi," Ruby Manfred whispered loudly. "He looks more like a *yeshiva bucher*."

The rabbi acknowledged that he had absolutely no acquaintance with or even the slightest knowledge of Herman Matterweil.

"It is clear from Herman Matterweil's life," intoned the rabbi, "that he was a leader, an inspiration, and a man who loved Israel. Almighty God, King of the Universe, it is not for us to know your plan. We may falter – we may ask ourselves why Herman Matterweil, our friend, our guide, the president of our co-op is no longer here. It is our task, our obligation, our spiritual duty to continue our lives, nay to rededicate our lives to the furtherance of the Jewish ideals and values which Herman Matterweil exemplified so well."

The rabbi glanced at his notepaper.

"The Olmsted Court Board of Directors wishes to express its grief," said the rabbi. "Speaking for the Board is Michael Levine."

Michael arose and walked stiffly up the aisle. He believed that he carried himself with a certain dignity; but as he walked he overheard at least one person who wondered if Michael had hemorrhoids.

Michael placed a set of index cards on the rostrum. Not daring to look at the people sitting in the chapel, Michael focused on the cards. He felt a sudden fatalistic calm, and began.

"When I learned that I was to speak here today, I was a bit surprised. I reacted the way I suspect some of you might have. Why Michael Levine? After all, Herman and I were not what you would call close. Then, I decided the choice was really appropriate.

"We are not here to play building politics. We are here to ponder the universal mystery of life and death. We are here to consider the limitations imposed by mortality. The fact that life as we know it is finite sometimes drives us to really silly behavior, and sometimes moves us, elevates us to make a statement that lasts beyond our days."

Now he looked up, and was taken aback by the way everyone looked at him as if they took him seriously. He noticed that Andre Castellano was sitting in an otherwise empty row.

"It is just and fitting," continued Michael, "that I who disagreed so much with Herman on a day-to-day basis am required to examine the whole man and share with you my admiration for his positive impact on our lives.

"Our home, Olmsted Court, was Herman Matterweil's passion. He transformed it from a building in which we happened to live to a special kind of community. A co-operative community. Shared work, shared responsibility, shared creation of an enterprise and an entity that truly is ours.

"When the landlord decided to bail out, it was Herman, first and foremost, who realized that we had an opportunity to take a more direct role in our separate and shared destinies. He discussed it in terms of business and investments. He could just as well have been talking about dignity and accomplishment. For that's what we have attained, thanks to Herman. Sure, we'll have our petty bickering — our disputes over repairs and what color to paint the lobby. But that's because we care. This ability and opportunity to care is also what Herman has given us.

"We know that a dollar value, an estimate of financial worth, can be assigned to each of our apartments. We must never forget that the idea of a co-op has as much or even more to do with the notion of self-worth. That is what Herman has given to us.

"We are here today to grapple with the mysteries of Herman Matterweil's mortality. What he has accomplished, what he has given to us, will endure. Let us hope that each of us can pass the same values, the same gifts, onto others.

"And so, although Herman and I were not friends, I am here today to pay him tribute. Thank you, Herman."

Michael put the index cards which he never looked at back into his pocket, and stepped down from the rostrum. Walking toward the chapel's rear, he felt hands clapping him on the back.

Michael passed the funeral parlor's office. The door was slightly ajar and Michael heard a familiar voice, the Rabbi's, obviously enmeshed in a phone conversation.

"Yes, Mommy, I said all those things you suggested. I mentioned Israel and leadership like you said. But nobody paid attention. I don't think there were any reporters here because nobody was taking notes.

"But mommy, I'm trying to tell you this other thing that happened. This guy spoke. He lives in the building, and everybody liked him better than they liked me.

"No, mommy. It's not my imagination. It's really true. Oh, by the way, did my mother call?"

Michael quickly stepped away from the office door and continued on his path toward the door. Walter grabbed him by the shoulder, and then shook his hand.

"Very good, Michael," said Walter. "Very good speech."

"Thank you," said Michael softly.

"You should have the honor of riding in the hearse with Herman. No two ways about it. You deserve it."

"I suppose I do," said Michael.

At least the driver won't tell me any jokes, he thought.

TEN

Handful of Soil

The hearse glided through traffic while the morning's rain slipped away.

A handful of people gathered at the gravesite. Sergeant Moscowitz studied the mourners from a respectful distance. The rabbi chanted the ancient words. Roberta Haven sniffed. Blanche Copra fidgeted. Krane crowded the gravesite. Calvin Birmingham stood like stone.

This is real, thought Michael. Herman Matterweil is dead. His body is in that coffin and I'm at his funeral. All I see are gravestones. Beneath some gravestones are the bodies of people who have been dead longer than I have been alive.

The rabbi raised his eyes from his Bible and peered straight at Michael.

"Mr. Levine, I suppose you have something you want to say again, some philosophical notions, some great truths to share with us."

"No," said Michael, "I didn't prepare any kind of re-marks."

"Ah," said the rabbi, "you didn't prepare anything. Very well."

Michael perceived a fat note of vindication in the rabbi's voice.

The casket was lowered. Each person tossed a handful of soil into the open grave. Krane looked at his wristwatch and hurried away.

The rabbi pronounced one more prayer and the service concluded.

As the mourners walked toward the cars, Michael caught up with the rabbi. Perhaps a fence could be mended.

"I want you to know," said Michael, "I was really taken by the things you said today. I was really in-spired."

"Don't patronize me," said the rabbi. "I know a hot dog when I see one."

The rabbi fired an Old Testament glare at Michael, and quickly stepped away.

"What did I ever do to that guy?" Michael asked Mos-cowitz who had appeared at his side.

"Come on," said the Sergeant, "I'll give you a ride back to your building."

Moscowitz was not a talkative driver. He seemed tuned out to everything but the road. At various points along the car's trajectory, Michael made astute observa-tions about the weather, the Long Island Expressway's many craters, and the many interesting experiences Moscowitz must have had in the course of his work. Mostly the Sergeant grunted in response.

As Sergeant Moscowitz and Michael Levine walked into Olmsted Court, two police officers, carrying over-stuffed cardboard cartons walked out of the building.

"What do you know," said Moscowitz, "we really are investigating."

"What's in those boxes?" asked Michael as the two walked into the elevator.

"We are gathering various of Mr. Matterweil's letters, papers, personal effects – so as to compile a more complete picture of the man and see if we can ascertain the identity or identities of any enemies."

The elevator stopped at the third floor, paused. shook, waited and slowly opened its door. Mrs. Florio stood in the corridor.

"Is it going down?" she asked.

"No," said Michael. "It's going up."

"Oh, too bad," said Mrs. Florio. "That was a wonderful speech you gave at Herman's funeral."

"Thank you," said Michael. "Those were just things that I thought should be said."

"I wasn't there," said Mrs. Florio; "but somebody else told me you were good.

"Thank you," said Michael.

The door closed.

"So," said Michael to Moscowitz, "I guess you'll be getting off at Herman's floor."

"Yes."

"I guess you've been checking Herman's apartment for fingerprints."

"Yes."

"And I guess you look for hair samples and stuff."

"Yes, we're always on the alert for stuff."

The door opened at the fifth floor, Herman's floor. Moscowitz stepped out and stood near apartment 5A, Herman Matterweil's apartment. Michael followed. A paper ribbon, bearing the words, "Keep out! This is the site of a police investigation," ran from the left side of the door to the right.

"Can I go inside and look around?" asked Michael.

"We don't really have our ticket booth set up," said Moscowitz.

Actually, Moscowitz was fond of letting civilians intrude once the forensic teams completed their work. Occasionally, they could spot an oddity he never would have noticed.

"I'll stay out of your way. Maybe I can help."

Moscowitz shrugged and pulled on the ribbon, making a path. He gestured, and Michael entered Herman's apartment.

Herman's apartment looked like it always did, except now it contained policemen who had made themselves at home. An "oldies" radio station emitted Otis Redding's version of "Try A Little Tenderness." Michael was sure that Herman never had heard this rendition.

At the dining room table, one police officer carefully placed papers into a cardboard box. While doing so, he sang along with Otis.

Michael looked into the living room and could not help but notice Herman's massive black leather chair. Now, the chair was occupied by a police officer who was eating a bologna sandwich with mayonnaise and lettuce on a seeded roll. A black attaché case sat to the right of the chair.

Herman always had exploited the chair's throne-like qualities. The vision of a seated Herman, grasping his calculator as if it were a scepter, flashed through Michael's mind. Michael grimaced.

"What's the matter?" asked Moscowitz.

"Nothing," said Michael. "I was just remembering something."

"What?"

"Herman's calculator," said Michael. Herman always had his calculator with him – especially when he sat on that chair."

"Ryan." said Moscowitz to the man eating the sandwich, "have you seen the vic's calculator anywhere?"

"No," Ryan said, and retuned to his sandwich.

"Officer Ryan," said Moscowitz, "this is Michael Levine. He's on the board of the co-op, and he's very interested in fingerprinting. Mr. Levine, Officer Ryan is our fingerprint specialist."

"No kidding," said Michael. "What made you get involved with fingerprinting?"

"Oh," said Ryan, "I thought I'd give it a whorl."

Michael looked at the police officer packing pieces of paper into the carton. He watched Ryan consume a bologna sandwich. He observed Moscowitz reviewing notebook entries.

"Are all investigations this boring?" asked Michael.

"We're trying to catch a murderer." said Moscowitz. "How can that be boring?"

"Have you come up with anything, yet?"

"We suspect foul play," said Ryan.

"Are you sure this is a police investigation?" asked Michael. "I mean you guys are the funniest thing since the Keystone Kops."

"I know this is your building," said Moscowitz, "but right now, you're on our turf which is where you wanted to be."

"I'm sorry," said Michael.

"Actually," continued Moscowitz, "we are beginning to develop a couple of theories. Judging from the undisturbed dust patterns on the surfaces, and the large quantity of money quite visible on top of his bedroom dresser, we feel robbery was not a motive. There are absolutely no signs of struggle nor are there the minutest traces of blood. We are fairly certain that the homicide was not committed in this apartment. It's likely that the murder, or at least Matterweil's dismemberment, occurred elsewhere, most likely in another apartment. Which means—" and he paused.

"Which means what?" asked Michael.

"Which means you probably have a very crazy person running around in this building."

"That's for sure," said Michael. "I just wonder which one of them actually killed Herman."

"I guess," Moscowitz continued, "you have seen a lot of crazy people in your time."

"The people I see are troubled. I'm uncomfortable with the term crazy.'"

"What kind of troubles do they have?"

"Fear, anger, shame, sorrow, guilt – the usual suspects."

"Are any of them angry enough to kill?"

Whoops, thought Michael.

"Wait a minute," said Michael, "Where are we going with this one?"

"As far as we can," said Moscowitz.

"If you're suggesting that any of my patients might have done this," said Michael, "you are way out in left field."

"Why?"

"Why? Why? Because it's ridiculous. That's why. I know these people. They're mixed up but they're not killers."

"Until I find the perpetrator, everyone's a suspect. If Mother Teresa had been seen entering or leaving this building, I'd want to know her whereabouts at the time of the murder."

"I'm a trained psychotherapist," said Michael. "Don't you think I would know if one of my patients had homicidal tendencies?"

"With all due respect, Mr. Levine, you do not specialize in the criminal mind. Even those of us who do often have to dig to find the perpetrator. I don't know if one of your people did it. And you don't know who did it either. But I'll tell you this: If it's not one of your patients, it's probably one of your neighbors. So the chances are that you are acquainted with the murderer. Perhaps your training will help you come up with a name. Meanwhile, you are, as we say in the trade, clueless."

"Yeah, well, if I do think of something, I will let you know," replied Michael, with as much dignity as possible.

"We are most appreciative," said Moscowitz.

"I've got to go now," said Michael.

"Thanks for dropping by."

I know the murderer, thought Michael, as he climbed the stairs to his apartment. I just don't know who the murderer is. What a way for Herman to die. Did we have to like Herman to care about the way he died? Did he know he was being killed? How did that feel? He must have been so lonely. Poor Herman. He gave us our home. And there's no family here. No friends. Just people like me who used to laugh at him or yell at him or hide from him. He was a person with a mind and a soul and a mommy. At least we can find out who did this. At least I can find out who did this. I have to. For Andre. For Herman. For me.

Herman has thrown one last curve at me. It was as if Herman were saying, "We know that you and I could not stand each other, and it is for just that reason that you must care about my death and how I died." This is not really fair.

ELEVEN

Out of Order

R ushing off to the 8:00 p.m. emergency board meeting, Michael scooped up a densely-typed single-spaced memo that apparently had been slipped under his door. The heading read "TO: Olmsted Court Shareholders. FROM: A Concerned Neighbor."

Michael, already late for the meeting, folded the page into quarters and slipped it into his back pocket.

In the basement, Michael walked through a dimly-lit corridor, dense with overhanging pipes and marked with doors that led to mysterious recesses. A sharp smell betrayed the presence of cats. The Board Room really was the building's laundry room. Clothes placidly tumbled in two of the six washing machines and all three dryers. The twin aromas of lemon-scented detergent and liquid bleach perfumed the air.

Michael took his seat at a long, folding, aluminum table that was chained to a pipe. The table was used mostly as a flat surface upon which people could sort and fold their laundry.

Walter Warren, Ethel Owens, and Blanche Copra already were in place. No one sat in Herman's seat. Michael wondered if Herman's ever-present calculator should have been placed at the empty spot in homage.

A seven-member Board governed the Olmsted Court Tenant Corporation. The other two surviving Boardmembers were Herb Vreeland, and Dr. Timothy Diamond. No one had seen Vreeland in eight months. Some asserted that the ever-absent Vreeland was an international, high-rolling businessman. Others thought he might be a bank-robber who plied his trade in other states. A third school held that Vreeland was a common garden-variety alcoholic who disappeared in order to dry out. Recently, Archie reported he had heard Vreeland had died under questionable circumstances in Tijuana. Nobody bothered to check this because monthly payments for Vreeland's apartment were up to date.

Dr. Diamond ran for the Board to represent shareholders who did not wish to get involved, and he received the largest number of votes. He attended the first Board meeting of the new term to make sure he was not elected to any office or appointed to any committee. His schedule apparently prevented him from attending any other meeting.

Walter Warren was the corporation's secretary/treasurer. His temperament seemed perfect for these responsibilities. A 46-year-old accountant, he allowed his occasional silences and gray temples to suggest the patient demeanor he hoped someday to attain. He found that dancing to someone else's choreography was soothing, and making his own decisions pure agony.

Blanche doodled on her legal pad. The few curving lines blossomed into a drawing of the Grand Army Plaza Soldiers and Sailors Monument. Usually, she etched scathing memos onto helpless lined paper.

"Perhaps we should wait just a few more minutes," said Walter.

"Ethel," said Blanche, "those are lovely earrings. That shade of green is just perfect for your eyes."

"Oh thank you," said Ethel, turning her head and beaming. "There's this lovely shop in Park Slope, and they have all kinds of wonderful stuff."

"I just love those stores," said Blanche.

"I know that place," said Michael. "They sell books there."

Ethel, Blanche and Walter looked at Michael for the first time and then quickly looked away.

"That note that got passed around," said Ethel, "really was not nice, Michael."

"I suppose you're right," said Michael.

"It was bad form," said Walter, "very bad form."

"You can't let these things get to you," said Michael. "There's always somebody out there, taking shots. The best thing to do is to ignore them."

"You're certainly taking this well," said Walter, for the second time in two days.

"Well, what's the choice?" asked Michael. "People always criticize the Board. We can't let it stop us. We've got too much work to do."

Walter, Ethel and Blanche exchanged glances.

"The jerk hasn't read it," said Blanche.

"I don't think name-calling is helpful," said Michael.

"This newest letter is not about the Board," said Blanche. "It's about you."

"It's about me?"

"It's the worst thing I ever read, Michael," said Ethel sweetly.

Michael slowly fished the page from his back pocket and read the contents. He knew the others were watching him so he tried hard for a poker face.

TO: Olmsted Court Shareholders

FROM: A Concerned Neighbor

Death has come to Olmsted Court in a cruel and vicious way. Our beloved leader Herman Matterweil was struck down by an assassin. What will happen to us now? Who will lead Olmsted Court to its place in the sun? Is someone else next?

Michael Levine may be able to answer the last question. Mr. Levine pretends he gets along with everybody. That ineffectual wimp routine he puts on is just that. It's an act! Nobody could really be that hopeless.

Why does he do it?

He brags about being a shrink. Would you brag about being in a profession where people exist only to get power over other people? Obviously he wants to have more power over Olmsted Court. Herman Matterweil stood in his way, and Herman is gone.

This is America! And nobody should make accusations without proof. I will therefore not accuse Michael Levine of killing Herman Matterweil. The murderer could just as easily have been one of Mr. Levine's crazy patients. It is a well-known fact that Herman Matterweil was deeply concerned about the many disturbed patients who visited Michael Levine and thereby gained access to our building. Herman was going to put a stop to it, and then he was murdered.

Let's honor Herman's memory. Let's prevent
Michael Levine from bringing any other homicidal
maniacs into the bosom of our building.

Michael refolded the page and returned it to his
pocket. He found Ethel, Blanche and Warren studying
him very carefully.

"Well," said Michael in a very even tone, "this certainly
is a hostile letter."

Oh God, he thought, I'm sunk. Somebody wants to
hurt me bad. Somebody wants to persecute my patients
and ruin my practice. I hope that cop doesn't see this.
Why are they doing this to me?

"And," he continued, "it's not good for the building.
Does anybody know who might have done this?"

There were no answers.

"Whoever did it is a sniveling coward," said Blanche,
"although I'm not thrilled about letting your patients into
our building. But that's a matter for another day."

First Herman, thought Michael, and now my reputa-
tion. And the building. Olmsted Court is being stalked.

"Do you think the killer might have written this note?"
asked Michael.

Walter glanced at his watch.

"You think," asked Blanche, "that somebody is man
enough to murder poor Herman, but can only go after you
with angry letters?"

"That's not what I mean," said Michael. "But the
chances are that one of our neighbors did Herman in
and—"

"Or one of your patients," said Blanche.

"Or that porter fellow," said Walter. "What's his
name?"

"Andre," said Ethel.

"I don't think it was Andre or one of my patients," said Michael, "but—"

"Of course, you're covering up for them," said Blanche.

"But," repeated Michael, "it was somebody and maybe we can put our heads together and try to figure out who."

"What do you want," asked Blanche, "a homicide committee? One more do-nothing committee?"

"No," said Michael, "of course not. But maybe if we think about this, we can come up with some ideas."

"Nobody is going to feel safe until the killer is found," said Ethel. "People are refusing to ride the elevator with each other. It's taking forever to go up or down."

"That's another reason to try to find the killer," said Michael.

"You've screwed up enough things on the Board," said Blanche, "I don't think you should expand your operation to police matters."

"I hope," said Walter, "we can finish relatively quickly. We basically only have one item on the agenda. I'd sort of like to get upstairs and see the National Geographic special."

"I just love that series," said Blanche. "I learn so much from it."

"It was just a thought," said Michael. "Perhaps we should start the meeting. Walter, I guess you should chair."

"Well, I don't know," said Walter.

"What's the big deal?" asked Blanche.

"I'm wondering if I'm empowered to act as chairman without authorization."

"That's easy," said Michael. "We'll vote on your being the chairman."

"But we can't vote," said Walter, "until the meeting is called to order. Only the chairman can call it to order. But if I have no authorization to chair, I can't declare a quorum is present."

"What does *Robert's Rules of Order* say?" asked Michael.

"How come this isn't covered in the Bylaws?" asked Blanche.

"I'm just worried about somebody not liking something we do," said Walter, "and suing me."

"Or maybe even us," said Ethel.

Yeah, right, thought Michael, you worry about who can call a meeting to order; but you don't care about the poison pen artist ruining my name in the building.

Michael arose from his chair and quickly walked to the laundry room's light switch. He thumbed the switch down and the room jumped into darkness.

"What the hell are you doing," said Blanche.

"Oh dear," said Ethel.

"The lights are out," said Walter.

"We don't know who's here," said Michael. "Maybe the whole elected Board is here. In fact, I think I heard somebody declare a quorum. Gee, it might be a good idea if Walter chairs the meeting. Does anybody object?"

There was silence.

"I guess," continued Michael, "Nobody objects. So..."

He turned the lights back on.

"Omigosh," said Michael, looking at one of the figures seated at the table. "Dr. Diamond, when did you get here?"

"Oh," said Diamond, "I've been around. Do you people always like to work in the dark?"

"If you'd been around more often," said Blanche, "you'd know that's a stupid question."

"I guess the meeting really has started," said Walter. "I'd like to dispense with the reading of the minutes due to the suddenness of this meeting."

"Now wait a minute," said Diamond, "I'm a board member and a shareholder. I must know what's going on. It's irresponsible to proceed without a reading of the minutes."

"If you really wanted to know what was going on," said Walter, "you'd make an effort to be here."

Walter frowned as if his reproof of Diamond were some sort of sudden heartburn.

"I don't have to explain myself to anybody," said Diamond. "I serve an important function in my own way."

A shopping cart's rusty creak signaled Mrs. Bloomfield's entrance. Wearing a powder blue house dress, the gray-haired woman wheeled her cart to dryer number two. She opened the dryer door, thrust her hand inside the belly-warm machine, and pinched various garments to see if there was any residual dampness. Satisfied, she slowly removed the dryer's contents.

"Please," said Walter," can we proceed?"

"Will you read the minutes?" asked Diamond.

"Are you making a motion?" asked Walter.

"I don't think a motion should be required to see that things be done in an orderly fashion."

"Mr. Chairman," said Blanche "point of information."

Mrs. Bloomfield pulled her cart over to the aluminum table and stared at the Board.

"What is it Blanche?"

"How long—"

"Point of order," said Diamond.

"Yes, Blanche, continue," said Walter.

"How long—"

"Mr. Chairman," insisted Diamond, "point of order takes precedence over point of information."

"Timothy, I already recognized Blanche, and I take precedence over you. Blanche, please, we'd like to hear what you have to say."

"Sure," said Blanche, "I just want to know how much longer you two jerks are going to waste our time with this nonsense."

"That's it," said Walter, "I'm not chairing anymore."

Quiet filled the room, except for washing machine number four, which went into the spin cycle. Michael took a black Pentel pen from his shirt pocket and examined it. Ethel surreptitiously popped two peppermint Chiclets into her mouth. Walter slowly rearranged the papers in his briefcase.

"Walter," said Michael, "you're doing a good job under difficult circumstances. Please continue."

Nobody else said anything. Walter was sufficiently persuaded that the silence indicated agreement.

"All right then," said Walter. "What with the sudden loss of Herman, we are obliged to select a new president."

"This," announced Diamond, "is something that should be decided by the shareholders."

"I really don't think so," said Walter, "I mean this is something the Board does."

Mrs. Bloomfield now concluded the Board was sitting pat; so she reached into her shopping cart, pulled out a half-dozen pastel-toned cotton garments, and started to fold a pair of peach panties. Blanche shouted, "There's no room here for that. There's no room. Take your stupid laundry and fold it in your damned apartment. There's no room."

Mrs. Bloomfield looked at the Board, and received no recognition. She returned the underwear to her cart, straightened her posture, and pulled her cart out of the laundry room. When the last creak no longer could be heard, Walter scratched his scalp.

"Perhaps, we can proceed now," said Walter

"Mr. Chairman," said Diamond, "this decision is too important to be decided by us."

"It's our job," said Michael.

"You're not considering the liability," said Diamond.

"Declare him out of order," said Blanche.

"I want," said Walter, "to make sure he understands—"

"But he's out of order."

"Blanche, please," said Walter.

"I'm making an important point," said Diamond.

"He's out of order," said Blanche.

"Liability," said Diamond.

"Out of order, out of order, out of order."

"Blanche, you're out of order," Walter declared.

"Maybe," said Ethel, "Dr. Diamond knows what he's talking about."

"Since when," snorted Blanche.

Ethel brought her left hand up to her right earlobe and absently touched the green earring Blanche had praised a few minutes earlier.

"The floor is open to nominations," said Walter.

"I nominate Dr. Timothy Diamond," said Ethel.

"I decline," said Diamond, "and if elected I will not serve. I represent an important constituency. I play an important role. I cannot have it hampered by something as trivial as the presidency."

"Especially," said Blanche dryly, "when you consider that the last president got killed."

"View it any way you wish," said Diamond. "I have spoken."

Diamond arose and glided out of the laundry room. When Dr. Diamond was no longer visible, Walter asked, "Nominations?"

"I nominate Walter Warren," said Michael.

"I decline," said Walter. "I don't think I can fill Herman's shoes. However, I nominate Ethel Owens."

"I decline," said Ethel. "No thank you."

"I want to do it," said Blanche. "I'll do it. I've wanted to straighten out this building for a long time."

"Blanche," said Michael, "are you really sure? Whoever killed Herman might want to kill the next president."

"Gee," said Walter, "that never occurred to me."

"Me neither," said Ethel. "I mean, not really."

"Don't be such wimps," said Blanche. "Lightning never strikes twice in the same place. Now let's get the show on the road. The first thing I want to do—"

"Excuse me," said Ethel, "I'm not that sure about the rules; but aren't we supposed to vote first?"

Blanche compressed her lips and shook her head in annoyance.

"I think Ethel has a valid point," said Walter. "Perhaps a formal nomination would also be in order. Therefore I nominate Blanche Copra for President."

"I second the nomination," said Ethel.

"Are there any other nominations?" asked Walter.

"Not on your life," said Ethel.

"I declare nominations closed," said Walter. "I instruct the secretary – me – to cast a vote for Blanche Copra. Congratulations Blanche."

"Yeah, thanks," said Blanche. "First of all, I want to thank you all for your deep confidence in me. Second of all, we're going to shake a few trees around here and see what falls out. We've done enough for tonight. Do I hear a motion to adjourn?"

"Yes," said Michael.

"So moved," said Walter.

"Let's adjourn," said Ethel.

The four sat back in their chairs for a moment. Walter looked at his wristwatch.

"What do you know," said Walter, "I'll be able to see the National Geographic special, after all."

"What's it about?" asked Ethel.

"I'm not sure," said Walter. "It's either about manatees or Manitoba. I just love their photography."

"Sounds interesting," said Michael.

Photography, thought Michael. Why am I wasting my life in a basement when I should be thinking about how to get more Dolores into my life?

"You know, Ethel," said Blanche, "one of these days you must take me over to that store in Park Slope. I'm always on the lookout for good earrings."

"Sure," said Ethel.

The four Boardmembers walked out of the laundry room together. Machine number four chugged to a stop.

Upstairs, Michael entered three items on his next day's to-do list.

1) Call Dolores.

2) Identify Herman's killer.

3) Get some fresh air.

TWELVE

Very Strong Predictions

Next morning Michael intensely studied his three-item to-do list.

I need to prioritize, he thought. Boy, it's stuffy in here. Fresh air, here I come.

Outside, Michael saw Roberta Haven kneeling in the garden in front of the building. People always had called the fenced-in patch of earth a garden; but Roberta made it bloom. Now she was methodically plucking weeds from the soil. Her right hand drifted laterally; stopped; lowered; gripped; and jumped upward. She dropped the captive weed into a cardboard carton, held by her left hand. Michael enjoyed the rhythm of her movement; and the sure motion of her hands.

Two joggers, a man and a woman, passed. Michael watched them pace their way along the sidewalk into the distance. They wore identical attire – orange tee shirts with triangular perspiration patches; gray running shorts; orange-striped white sweat socks; and Nike running shoes.

(Michael once had referred to such shoes as sneakers, and was rebuked in detail by the wearer.) The joggers wore orange sweat bands and grey headbands. Without exchanging words or looks, they moved in tandem – sometimes drifting to the left, sometimes to the right.

Michael drank in the scene and returned to the lobby. As he neared Archie's station, Blanche stomped past him and went outside. Calvin Birmingham followed.

"Guess what?" Archie boomed.

"What?" Michael asked tamely.

"I know a guy who works in another building," said Archie, "and he said plumbers are refusing to make repairs here unless they've got armed guards. Because of Mr. Matterweil's um – you know – murder."

"Wait a minute," yelled Michael. "Archie!"

"Yes?"

"What are you telling people?"

"I just heard that plumbers refuse to work here without—"

"I don't want to hear it," said Michael.

"But you just asked."

"'What are you telling people' doesn't mean 'what stories are you telling people.' I don't want to know what you're saying to people. I want to know why you're saying these things."

"Why didn't you say 'why'?"

"Come on, Archie, I didn't have to say 'why.' I said 'what,' and in this case 'what' meant 'why.'"

"Forgive me Mr. Levine. I only had two years of high school."

"It's got nothing to do with high school. It's an expression. It's like another expression – 'What are you talkin'?' Have you ever heard that one?"

"So, you didn't want to hear what I was telling him?"

"Exactly."

"If you say so. I guess that means you don't want to hear the other stories."

"Other stories?"

"Yeah, about Mr. Matterweil's murder."

"And you've been passing these stories on to people in the building?"

"If I know something," said Archie, "I think I should share it. After all, everybody's been so good to me."

"What are you telling people?" asked Michael.

"I got you, Mr. Levine," said Archie. "You want to know why I'm telling people these things."

"No," said Michael. "I want to know what. I want to know what you're telling them."

"You do?"

"Yes!"

"You're sure?"

"Yes!!"

"I'm just telling them the things I hear."

"Like what?"

"Like Olmsted Court being bankrupt."

"It's not!"

"That's what I tell them," said Archie. "I tell them this is what I heard; but it's probably not true."

Michael spoke very slowly and through clenched teeth.

"It's not true at all," said Michael.

"Well, that's a load off my mind," said Archie.

"What else," said Michael. "What else do you tell them?"

"The other thing I heard," said Archie, "and I heard this from someone who ought to know, is that Mr.

Matterweil's enemies are going to blow up Olmsted Court."

"We don't even know who Matterweil's enemies are," said Michael.

"Ain't that something," said Archie. "Doomed to explode. You know it's going to happen; but you don't know who's going to do it."

"It's not going to happen," said Michael. "There's a very strong likelihood that Herman Matterweil's killer lives in this building. Whoever he is, he's not going to blow up the building."

"Boy," said Archie, "people will really be glad to hear that."

"Stop telling things to people," said Michael.

"But people trust me," said Archie. "I got my position to think of."

"These stories aren't true," said Michael exasperatedly. "They're rumors."

"Yes, Mr. Levine," said Archie in sing-song fashion.

Michael turned and walked toward the elevator.

"Wow," said Archie, "Look at them."

"Look at who," said Michael, without turning around."

"Blanche Copra and Birmingham. They're really going at it."

Michael stopped, turned and looked outside. Blanche Copra's face was twisted into pure anger. Calvin Birmingham's face displayed more shock than anger. Although Birmingham was easily a foot-and-a-half taller than the new co-op president, he was shaken by her fury. It seemed to Michael that Blanche didn't even care about the effects of her hostility. There was something almost kamikaze-like about the way she tore into the superintendent. Michael moved toward the outside and Archie swung the front door open.

"Those apartments have to be repaired," said Calvin. "That's the way Mr. Matterweil wanted it."

"I'm the president now," said Blanche, spitting the words out. "And I'll decide who gets repairs and who doesn't. If you don't like it, you can get yourself another job."

She turned away from Birmingham, and walked toward Michael.

"I'll be here after you're gone," said Birmingham.

Blanche stopped, paused, turned around, and stared at Birmingham. With a very even cadence, she said, "Don't count on it, you moron."

She turned again, and walked inside. As she passed Michael, Blanche said, "I've got something for you too. It's under your door."

Michael walked over to Calvin Birmingham and, in his most therapeutic voice, said, "I think she's under a lot of stress."

"That wasn't stress," said Calvin, "that was pure unadulterated bitch. She shouldn't have talked to me like that. That's no way to talk to anybody."

"It'll work out," said Michael. "You'll see."

"Old man Matterweil is dead and she's still breathing," said Calvin. "That ain't right."

Michael decided he had done all he could for this situation, so he went back inside.

Blanche's memo, stuck under Michael's door, seemed to be tapping its foot impatiently. Michael sat down in the old living room armchair and subjected himself to Blanche's note.

TO: BOARD OF DIRECTORS

FROM: BLANCHE COPRA, YOUR NEW PRESIDENT

Olmsted Court is in trouble, and we're going to save it. I decided Michael Levine made a good point. It's our job as a Board to assist the police in bringing Herman's murderer to justice. But it takes more than talk. I am creating an investigation committee to help the cops. This committee is empowered to do anything necessary to dig up facts – question shareholders, look at records, turn names over to the cops. I'm naming Michael Levine as the committee chairman. You can begin by checking the arrearage records. Anybody behind in their maintenance payment is a suspect. Make up a list of these people and give that list to the cops, etc. Don't worry about your patients. I'll have somebody else take care of that.

I am calling for a special shareholder's meeting to take place tomorrow night. I think it's right for the shareholders to learn of and meet their new president. Also, we'll discuss the unpleasant situations revolving around Herman's death. We'll get rid of some nasty rumors being spread. Archie tells me people are saying all sorts of things.

That's all for now.

Investigations committee, thought Michael. I guess that was my idea. But the way she lays it out, it sounds so mean. Arrearage records! She's making it sound like an economic crime. Marjorie accused me of not being close enough to life. I hope she's happy.

The telephone's sudden sharp ring cut into Michael's thoughts. Could it be Dolores?

"Hello, Michael, this is Walter."

"Oh, hello Walter."

"Listen, I'm at work; so I really can't spend too much time on the phone. I've been informed .that Blanche and Calvin had an argument."

"Already?" asked Michael. "They were yelling at each other only a few minutes ago. It just happened. People called you already? I'm impressed."

"Then, there really was an argument?" asked Walter.

"Yes," said Michael.

"People told me there were threats," said Walter.

"I didn't hear the whole discussion," said Michael.

"Were there threats?"

"Things were said in the heat of the moment; but I wouldn't really call them threats."

"What would you call them?"

"Very strong predictions. But Blanche threatens everybody. Been doing it for years."

"Do you mean Calvin didn't say anything of a menacing nature?"

"I suppose he said a couple of things he shouldn't have; but I wouldn't really call them threats."

"Hmm," said Walter, "I don't want to have to look for a new super now. If you hear anything else about this, let me know."

"I don't have your phone number at work," said Michael.

"I'd better give it you," said Walter, "but I have to get off the phone right now. I'll talk to you later. Keep me posted." –CLICK-

"Okay," said Michael to the dead phone.

At least I can find out who did this. I have to. For Andre. For Herman. For me.

THIRTEEN

Some Little Breakthrough

Dolores Caruso, wearing a pale green tee shirt and baggy khaki shorts, bent over a U-shaped white work table that she had built. Piles of black-and-white proof sheets cluttered the surface. Dolores loved the way images from a single roll of film fit on a single 8 1/2" x 11" contact sheet. It made her feel she was looking into the soul of a shoot. Bold red strokes from China red marking pencils splashed across each sheet.

Dolores was looking at a contact of Granny Abbott the quiltmaker. Granny combined appliqués, designs and stitches to tell the story of her family. Three images of Granny Abbott sewing a rabbit appliqué onto the quilt attracted Dolores; but she didn't know which to use. The phone rang and the answering machine picked up.

"Hello," said the machine, "this is Dolores Caruso. I am probably out on assignment. If your call is urgent, please page me at—"

Maybe, she thought, I should use the third one. It shows everything so clearly. But it's duller than the others. Maybe I should print up all three and decide later. No, if I start working that way, then, I'll never be finished.

"—and I'll get back to you."

The machine beeped. The caller spoke hesitantly.

"Hello, hello. This is Michael. I want to apologize. I hope you'll return my call. I would like to apologize to you face-to-face or phone-to-phone for—"

Dolores placed a magnifier over the sharp, static image and grabbed the phone.

"This is Dolores."

"Thank you for picking up. I was a real fool the other night and I am so upset at what I did. I apologize for the damage I caused and just the total lack of respect. I hope you can forgive me."

This is the moment of truth, thought Dolores. I can push him away or I can see where this is going to go. Where do I want it to go? I don't know; but I guess I want it to go somewhere.

"I appreciate this call very much, Michael."

"I don't think I've behaved like that since I was 15 years old."

"Oh?"

"Something else was going on," he said and he told her about Herman.

"I can see," she said slowly, "how that might affect your judgment."

Who, wondered Michael, is the therapist here?

"Yes," he said. "No, the weirdness was all mine. I enjoyed being with you so much that I wanted it to keep on going. I didn't have the brains or sensitivity to pay attention to your needs."

"I had a good time, too, until – until—"

"Until I ruined your dress and broke that beautiful glass."

"Um, things did take a turn at that point."

"Oh, God, let me pay for the dry cleaning and the glass. I'm really sorry."

"Listen, Michael, I really do accept your apology. You don't have to say you're sorry anymore."

Sunshine splashed through the clouds in Michael's head.

"Thank you," said Michael.

"You're welcome," said Dolores.

"Great," said Michael. "So now what?"

Michael pictured Dolores at the other end of the phone. Her long fingers probably toyed with her curly blonde hair as she spoke.

"Now what?" Dolores echoed.

"When can I see you again?"

"He is cute, thought Dolores. She took a deep breath, surprised at her own quick response.

"The fact is," she said, "I've gotten a lot done the last couple of days, and I was going to reward myself with a long lunch. Would you care to join me?"

Michael gazed adoringly at Dolores as she deftly nibbled at a cannoli in the Cafe Roma, an espresso house in Manhattan's Little Italy. In the background, cappuccino machines hissed and tourists approvingly "ooed and ahhed" ogling brightly colored pastries in the display counter. Michael picked at his Napoleon. It was hard to look sophisticated while eating gooey desserts.

Michael tried not to stare at Dolores. He contemplated the roundness and imagined warmth of her breasts, hiding inside her pale blue blouse. He followed the path from the tip of her pinkie to wrist to elbow to her shoulder. The pale wisp of underarm hair peeking out of the short sleeve of her blouse enthralled him.

He felt concentric waves of affection rocking him. He cherished every word Dolores breathed in his direction. Was it possible to be sensitive and supportive to a woman and still obsess about her nipples?

"How long have you known the Meachams?" asked Michael.

"About 10 years," said Dolores. "I was doing a project about high school. I wanted to document the high school experience — not the myth that I remembered; but the reality that kids were going through. Juliet was a teacher at the first school I went to. She helped me get through the bureaucracy. She introduced me to some kids; so they accepted me. She was absolutely marvelous and we became friends."

"They're great people," said Michael. What did you ever do with those pictures?"

"Oh," said Dolores. "I had an exhibit that was in New York, Philadelphia, Chicago and Los Angeles. People bought prints. The most popular image was of a teenaged couple necking in a study hall."

"Wait a minute," said Michael, "I've seen that picture. It's very good."

"Thank you," said Dolores.

"You're welcome," said Michael.

"*Newsweek* used some pictures; and different magazines and now newspapers run one of the pictures every time there's a new high school scandal or some official education report."

"So, you're still earning money from it," said Michael. "It sounds like a satisfying way to make a living."

"I enjoy it," said Dolores. "But it's no way to make a living. I spent four solid years on it."

"Why so long?" asked Michael.

"The more I learned," said Dolores, "the greater the number of subjects I had to shoot. The more I shot, the more I learned.

"The funny thing," she continued, "is that I thought it would only take a few months of my time, and that I would get a lot of money in return. This is nothing. Other projects have taken longer with less remuneration."

"That sounds pretty grim," said Michael. "Do you ever feel like walking away from it?"

"Once in awhile," said Dolores. "But you know the old joke – 'What? Give up show business?' I love my work. It's thrilling. It's special, and sometimes I even have a slight impact on the world. You should understand that. Don't you have the same thing?"

"I guess so," said Michael, "When you take a new patient you say what an interesting case. How lucky she is or he is that they've come to you. You know exactly what you're going to do to help this person. You start treating the patient, and nothing works. You're in a rowboat in the middle of the ocean, and there are no stars to steer by. Then, there's some little breakthrough. The patients yell at you or have an incredible crying jag during the session, or suddenly announce some insight that they rejected three months earlier. Maybe the patient starts paying more attention to his or her appearance.

"Whatever it is, there's some kind of breakthrough. You're reminded that this is a long process, and you're here to help the patient – not vice versa. It's important to be reminded of why you're here."

"What do you mean?"

"Ego," said Michael. "The therapist's ego. My ego. This field is saturated with ego. The patient responds to me. I give the patient a new life. I am the important one in this process. My needs and desires must come first."

"How do you avoid that?"

"You don't. You can't. You just hope that you remember that the ultimate goal is to help people. Right now I remember what a patient just said — that the closest I come to life is listening to other people's stories. She might be right. But if you're helping people for all the wrong reasons, well, at least you're still helping people.

"I don't know if I work at helping people," Michael continued, "because I genuinely want to, or because I'm trying to please my parents. They always insisted that I make friends, and that I share what I had with other people. It may have propelled me into a helping profession; but at the same time I can be really selfish. It doesn't express itself in material greed. I work hard at being thoughtful; but I still manage to be thoughtless in so many ways. Ellen always got pissed off at the way I made appointments for the two of us without consulting her."

"Ellen?"

"She's my – uh – she was my – uh—"

"Girlfriend?" asked Dolores.

"We broke up a couple of months ago. Or rather, she walked out on me."

"That's tough," said Dolores.

"The tough part," said Michael, "is that I cared about her so much, and yet I had trouble showing it."

"Isn't it hard to show affection to somebody who's always getting pissed off at you?"

"Who's the shrink around here? That's a good observation but I really did drive her away."

"How did you do that?"

"I just wouldn't be what she wanted me to be."

"Wouldn't or couldn't?"

"What's the difference?"

"There's a difference," said Dolores, "especially if you believe there's such a thing as people being right for each other."

"Do you believe there's such a thing as people being right for each other?" asked Michael.

"Absolutely," said Dolores; "but it's like believing in God. It's all faith, and no evidence."

"What about us?" asked Michael. "Do you believe we might be right for each other?"

"Today has been pretty good," Dolores said. "Perhaps."

Michael caught the waitress's eye and with constricted throat muscles croaked the words, "check, please."

It was a slow, sweetly agonizing walk from the Cafe Roma to Dolores's loft.

I'm falling, she thought. What happens when I hit the ground?

They continued on their path.

As soon as the loft door closed behind them, Michael and Dolores embraced. They stood in an endless sway.

"Dolores," Michael murmured, "may I take a giant step?"

"Yes," she replied, "Yes, you may."

Michael found Dolores's lips and the unbearable tension he had so long hoped for. The sweet liquid kisses seemed to flow for an eternity. They paused, gazing at one another. They kissed once more.

"I'll bet you have some work to do," said Michael.

"I didn't quite know how to work it into the conversation, but yes."

"I will call you later," he said.

"Yes," she said.

FOURTEEN

On the Fritz

The Olmsted Court lobby sizzled with whispered rumors as shareholders gathered for the 8:00 p.m. special meeting. Walter and Ethel sat at the card table that represented leadership and authority. Michael meandered through groups of two and three shareholders studded throughout.

"Hey Levine," called Krane the salesman, "congratulations."

Oh no, thought Michael, somebody told Krane about my date with Dolores.

"I hear you've been promoted to Chief Inspector," said Krane. "It's all over the building how you're in charge of finding Herman's killer. Are you going to swear in deputies?"

"Deputies?" asked Michael.

"Or are ya gonna track the bad guys by yourself cuz a man's gotta do what a man's gotta do. We must be the only co-op in New York with an Investigations Committee, and you're the Chairman."

"Chairperson," said Michael automatically.

"Forgive me," said Krane, "Old habits die hard. Chairperson of the Investigations Committee. You know, I had a friend—"

"No," said Michael, "I don't want to hear one of your jokes that starts out with 'I had a friend.' Not this time. Not tonight."

"No, really," said Krane. "I had a friend who was a bailiff and he swore people in at trials. Once, there was this witness, a big-shot Senator or something, and my friend said, 'Do you swear to tell the truth, the whole truth and nothing but the truth, so help you God?' The Senator said, 'my good man, I'll have you know I've been an elected official for 27 years.'"

Michael walked away; but Krane pursued, "and my friend said, 'that's exactly why we have to ask that question.'"

"Mr. Levine!"

The sound of jangling bracelets meant that Evelyn Ross had a complaint. Her bony forefinger, adorned by a turquoise and silver ring, pointed straight at Michael.

"The elevator is acting up, Mr. Levine," said Ross, "and I want you to do something about it right now."

"What do you mean it's acting up?"

"It skipped my floor four times, both going up and going down. The only reason I'm here in the lobby is that I finally decided to try to get the elevator on the floor below."

"Good thinking," said Michael.

Lucky us, he thought.

"Never mind good thinking," she said. "The elevator is on the fritz, and I want you to fix it."

"I left my tools upstairs," said Michael.

Evelyn Ross frowned. It was not a pretty sight.

"Mrs. Ross," said Michael, "the thing to do is to report the problem to the elevator repair company. Right over there is the table where Board members sit. Walter and Ethel are there already. Blanche should be down any second now. She's the new president, and I'm sure this is something she'll want to handle personally."

"Just when do you expect her majesty to get down here?"

"The meeting is called for eight o'clock," said Michael.

"It's after eight already; but she always has to make a grand entrance. Now that she's grabbed the president thing, she's going to be more insufferable than ever. I guess we'll hear trumpets announcing her arrival."

"I thought you two were friends," said Michael

"Of course, we're friends," said Evelyn Ross. "We're very close; but that doesn't stop me from knowing she's a real witch."

"Maybe," Krane's voice roared, "she'll fix the elevators herself by waving her magic wand."

"Mr. Krane," said Evelyn Ross, "don't you have any of your own business to mind?"

"No," said Krane, "and I had a friend who never minded his own business and—"

"I'm not surprised in the least," said Ross who turned on her heel and walked away.

"This friend never minded his business, see," said Krane to Michael.

"I'm sure he came to a disgusting end," said Michael who also walked away.

"I believe," said Krane to no one in particular, "that this building has a real sense of humor problem."

The murmurs of the milling residents had cascaded. Michael estimated that maybe 50 of his neighbors were now pacing the lobby floor. A dozen or so people surrounded the flimsy card table where Walter Warren still sat. Ethel had disappeared. Jeremiah Gordon derisively pointed his finger at Walter.

"Was this meeting not called for eight o'clock," demanded Gordon.

"Yes, it was," Walter glumly admitted.

"And it now is 27 minutes past the hour of eight. Is it not?"

"Well," said Walter, "my watch says 8:24; but —"

"I submit to you," said Gordon, "that whether it is 8:27, as indicated by my fine timepiece which has been a reliable instrument since first purchased 35 years ago as many people here can attest, or it is 8:24 as you allege, my valuable time and that of our friends and neighbors has been wasted. We'll never get that time back because you people have been inefficient."

The people ringing the table nodded approvingly.

"Such a great man," said Mrs. Buxbaum.

"Yes," said Michael dryly. "At least 11 murderers and eight leaders of organized crime owe their freedom to his efforts in their behalf."

"Truly a great man," said Mrs. Buxbaum.

"My time is worth $200 an hour," said Jeremiah Gordon, "and many of our friends and neighbors, gathered here, regularly charge for their time. If we were to bill you collectively for the aggregate of our wasted time that would be quite a hefty sum."

"Now, Jerry, come on —" Walter began.

"Nobody is allowed to call me 'Jerry' except for judges. In fact, now that I'm retired they can't call me by that name either."

"Jeremiah," said Walter, "You know I agree with you about punctuality. The meeting — especially this meeting — really shouldn't start until Blanche gets here. She is the new president, and it just makes sense for her to chair from the beginning. And you know how Blanche is. She's never been able to get to a shareholders' meeting on time. I think it's because she's so shy."

"An interesting observation," said Gordon, "but I believe I've made my position clear."

Jeremiah Gordon strode toward a neutral corner, and was followed by most of the people who ringed the card table.

"Walter," said Michael, "did I hear you say Blanche is shy?"

"Well, yes," said Walter. "In a manner of speaking, I'd say she is shy."

"Where is she? This is her meeting."

"She's always late to shareholder meetings," said Walter.

"And early to Board meetings," said Michael.

"I asked Ethel to go and see if she could sort of hurry Blanche down," said Walter.

As he said this, Ethel could be seen making her way to the table.

"Where's Blanche?" asked Ethel.

"I thought you were getting her," said Michael.

"She isn't here," said Walter.

"I rang her bell," said Ethel, "and I knocked on her door, and there was no answer. By the way, the elevator is not working. I think it's stuck on the fourth floor. I had to walk down."

"Maybe it will be fixed by the time the meeting is over," said Walter. "Maybe Blanche just didn't hear you."

Walter, Ethel and Michael suddenly became aware of screams of outrage and despair in the background, as news of the injured elevator spread.

"I was at her door quite a few minutes, just ringing and knocking," said Ethel.

"Maybe she was writing a memo, and ran out of venom," said Michael.

"Uncalled for," said Walter.

"I gave it a try," said Ethel, "and that's that. I'm going to sit down now."

She slipped back into her chair at the table. A clanking of chains and creaking of gates announced the lobby floor arrival of the freight elevator. Andre, the porter, tightly secured the three large green plastic trash bags that sat in the corner. He opened the freight elevator's gate, stepped onto the lobby's floor, closed the gate behind him, and casually sauntered over to the card table.

"At least the freight elevator is running," said Walter. "If the regular elevator is down, we can use the freight elevator as an alternate."

Andre stared first at Walter, then at Ethel, and then Michael. He stepped toward Michael, and then, with a look of complete despair, planted himself near Walter. He cupped his hand about his mouth, leaned toward Walter, and whispered in Walter's ear. Walter's eyes and mouth opened wide.

"Excuse me folks," he said to Michael and Ethel. "I'll be back in a couple of minutes. Michael, would you please get the meeting started?"

"What about Blanche?" asked Michael.

Walter turned his gaze toward the freight elevator. Michael's eyes and Ethel's eyes followed. They stopped at the overstuffed trash bag in the elevator's corner.

Michael's eyes widened.

"Do you mean," began Ethel.

Walter nodded.

"All three bags?" asked Michael.

"Just the one in the corner, this time," said Walter.

Andre listlessly wandered to a corner of the lobby, sat on the floor, pulled his knees up, and put his head on his knees.

"Ladies and gentlemen," said Michael, "we're starting the meeting."

"Where's Blanche," wondered Evelyn Ross.

"It doesn't look like she's going to be able to make it," said Michael.

"This is her meeting," said Ross. "You have no right to take it over."

Evelyn Ross stomped over to the passenger elevator, and poked her knotty thumb at the call button. There was no response.

"Mr. Levine," shouted Evelyn Ross, "before you act like a big shot, do something real like getting the elevator fixed."

"But Evelyn—" said Michael.

"Don't you dare 'But Evelyn' me. I came down for Blanche's meeting. I'm not going to waste my time with you."

She marched over to the freight elevator, flung the gate wide open, and stepped inside.

"Get somebody to run this thing," Ross bellowed. "I want to go home. Also get these bags out of here. I don't travel with trash."

She tugged at one bag, alternately pushing, pulling and lifting it out of the freight car. She turned her attention to the next bag; but had difficulty in lifting it.

"No Evelyn," said Michael.

"No," chorused Ethel and Walter.

"What do people in this building throw out," wondered Evelyn Ross. "Somebody come here and give me a hand."

As if on cue, the bag opened. Out popped an arm, with its blood-painted hand pointing straight at Evelyn Ross. Evelyn screamed hysterically. Hearing Evelyn Ross, Olmsted Courters rushed over to the freight elevator. Seeing the trash bag and its partially revealed contents, the shareholders abruptly stopped, wheeled and ran in the other direction. From the thick of the crowd, Jeremiah Gordon's distinctive voice boomed.

"That's it," he announced. "I'm suing."

Anonymous voices agreed.

They're in panic, thought Michael.

"Ladies and gentlemen," said Michael, "It would be good to have our meeting. It would be good to confront and share our feelings."

There was a palpable pause as everyone thought this over.

"It would be good," said Krane the salesman, "to get the hell out of here."

The crowd of shareholders flowed back toward the freight elevator.

"Andre," Walter called to the porter. "Take people up."

Now that it was an official emergency, the populace performed well. They did not try to squeeze into the freight elevator. Their urgent need to retreat to the haven of their own apartments was tempered by their respect for Blanche Copra's remains, and their fear of disaster caused by exceeding the freight elevator's weight limits.

Michael, Walter and Ethel watched silently as their neighbors somberly filed onto the freight elevator, and allowed themselves to be ferried up. Walter was the first to speak.

"I think," said Walter, "that under the circumstances, it's all going well."

"Yes," said Ethel, "under the circumstances."

Michael was silent.

"Michael, don't you think it's going well," asked Walter, "under the circumstances?"

"If," responded Michael, "the circumstances you refer to include the facts that Herman was killed, and a few days later, tonight, Blanche was killed, and the person or persons who killed them have not been captured, and the elevator doesn't work, and this co-op's stability is being seriously threatened, I would say 'yes, we're doing swimmingly.'"

There was silence again, and the three watched the last bunch of apartment-bound shareholders.

"I guess we can go up now," said Walter.

"I think we've waited long enough," said Ethel.

"Aren't we forgetting something?" asked Michael.

The other two looked at him blankly.

"Now that Blanche is gone we need another president. We've got to decide among ourselves and elect another president."

"I suppose you're right," said Walter, "but we can't elect somebody to a position where they might get killed. Let's draw straws instead. Short straw is it."

"No," said Michael sharply. "We mustn't select a president that way. Of course, this is a very serious crisis. But the normal emergencies have to be tended to. We asked to be permitted to serve. We were elected on that basis. Our choice of president is important. We can't just abdicate our responsibilities. Too many people depend on us."

"Michael is right about responsibility," said Ethel. "I nominate Michael."

"Wait a minute," said Michael. "Nobody has ever thought I was right for the job."

"We never understood until now," said Walter. "You did mean what you said, didn't you?"

"Well, yes," said Michael.

"Okay," said Walter. "I second the nomination. Are there any other nominations? Not hearing any, I close nominations. As secretary, I cast a vote for Michael."

"Walter," wondered Michael, "aren't you usually concerned about things like quorums and such."

"Yeah," said Walter, "I can be such a fuddy-duddy. But I don't think anyone will challenge this action. Congratulations, Michael, and best of luck. I really mean it."

"Can we adjourn?" asked Ethel.

"Why not," said Michael.

The three walked slowly to the freight elevator. Michael walked the slowest.

FIFTEEN

Only in America

Three blue-and-white patrol cars, one orange-and-white ambulance and Sergeant Moscowitz's dark green Pontiac double-parked along the Eastern Parkway service road. Fiery red, icy blue, and glaring white lights revolved atop the vehicles and lent a hush to the street.

When Michael Levine heard the shrill sirens approach, crescendo, then suddenly stop, he returned to the lobby, filled with the hum of soft voices. Sergeant Moscowitz and Officer Tatum spoke with Fred the night doorman. Another police officer questioned Andre, who still sat sadly in the corner. Two paramedics, in whites, leaned against the wall near the freight elevator and talked about movies they recently had rented. Also leaning against the wall was the green trash bag containing Blanche Copra's body. Michael walked toward the green bag.

Moscowitz suddenly cut across the lobby to pass in front of Michael. The sergeant wore tan chinos; and a bright green shirt under a brown sportcoat. Two dog-walking Olmsted Courters sauntered outside.

Moscowitz stuck out his huge, meaty hand, and he and Michael ceremoniously shook hands.

"I should learn not to have a bowling night," said Moscowitz. "I would have been here a couple of minutes sooner, except that the bowling alley made me return their shoes."

"Can't you arrest them for that," asked Michael, "or give them a ticket or something?"

"To tell the truth," said Moscowitz, "I could do without investigating a homicide while wearing bowling shoes. I'd never hear the end of it."

"Blanche is in that bag," said Michael, pointing toward the freight elevator.

"Yes," said Moscowitz.

Michael walked toward the freight elevator.

"Wait a minute," said Moscowitz.

"You take your Martin Scorcese," said the taller paramedic, "he really takes care of details."

Michael paused at the trash bag.

"Don't," commanded Moscowitz.

"I already saw Herman's head," said Michael, as he pulled the flap aside, "so what—" and he saw Blanche's face, only it wasn't her face. The killer had battered Blanche with such force that Michael found himself looking at a gruesome assemblage of bone, skin, and glistening blood where he knew the woman's face ought to be.

Michael suddenly felt lightheaded. The whole lobby seemed to disappear. Michael felt himself teetering. Just as his numb legs were about to give way, everything came back into focus.

"Oh my God," said Michael.

"Why don't you sit down," said Moscowitz.

"No, it's okay," said Michael. "Is that the kind of stuff you see all the time?"

"It varies," said Moscowitz. "Why did you have to go and look at it?"

"I just felt I should."

"I think," said the shorter paramedic, "that this was his first stiff."

"No kidding," said the taller of the two. "Wait till he sees *Reservoir Dogs*."

"I understand you're the new president, here," said Moscowitz.

"It's true," said Michael.

"Are you crazy?"

Tatum joined Sergeant Moscowitz and Michael Levine.

"Sergeant," said Tatum.

"What?!"

"Do you want what we have so far?"

"Shoot!"

"The deceased, Blanche Copra, was found by the porter, Andre Castellano at approximately 8:15 p.m. Castellano was in the basement making his rounds when he tripped across the bag containing Copra. He placed the bag inside the elevator and began his rounds. He hoped he would come in contact with the superintendent, Calvin Birmingham; but Birmingham apparently was not on the premises."

At the mention of Calvin's name, Michael recalled the argument he and others had witnessed.

"Sergeant," said Michael.

"Just a minute."

"There was some sort of tenants' meeting going on in the building," Tatum continued, "and Castellano gave up on trying to find the super. So he told the tenants about the little package he was carrying.

"Time of death is estimated at about six p.m. She was beaten severely about the head and face with a blunt instrument. It was a blow to the head that sent her bye-bye. There are no signs of struggle and no signs of sexual attack. There's no blood in the basement where the body bag was found. We think the actual homicide took place somewhere else in the building. We're checking the walls and corridors to see what floor the body was taken from."

"What about Birmingham?" asked Moscowitz. "Where is he?"

Tatum shrugged.

"I wanted to tell you about Calvin," said Michael. "He and Blanche had a very intense argument this afternoon."

"Yeah," said Moscowitz. "She called him a moron and he threatened her."

Moscowitz noticed Michael's surprised expression.

"Hey, we're the police," the sergeant explained. "Tell me, did Blanche Copra have any romantic entanglements within the building?"

"Are you kidding?" asked Michael.

Moscowitz glared.

"Not that I know of," said Michael"

"Tatum," said Moscowitz, "are you sure that she had no sexual attack or sexual relations near the time of death."

"That's what Doc says. "

Moscowitz shook his head.

"What's the big deal?" asked Michael.

"She was killed by having her head bashed in," said Moscowitz. "It was only after that the perpetrator beat the woman's face into a bloody pulp."

"So?"

"This kind of thing happens in some sex-related murders," said Moscowitz.

"Really?"

"I thought you were a shrink."

"A psychotherapist, yes."

"In some cases," said Moscowitz, "the killer has performed a sex act that conflicts with his deeply felt self-image regarding sexual conduct. He turns the anger he feels toward himself outward toward the victim. After the murder he destroys the victim's face so as to literally erase a witness to the particular sexual act."

"I knew that," said Michael. "I just haven't looked at that literature lately."

"Of course," said Moscowitz.

The taller paramedic joined the conference.

"So you think this is a sex murder?" Michael asked.

"There is that business about the face."

"I don't think Marjorie had any kind of sexual or romantic relationship," said Michael.

"Marjorie?"

"I'm sorry. I meant Blanche."

"Who's Marjorie?"

"A patient of mine. I wonder why I said Marjorie. It must have been the anger. Marjorie has an awful lot of rage; but you were talking about the murderer's anger. If anything, Marjorie's anger tends to provoke other people into hurting her."

"So, she's not capable of hurting other people?"

"I didn't say that. She can be quite sarcastic."

"What about physically?"

"I don't think so."

"'I don't think so' is not the same as 'no.' Has Marjorie ever expressed concern about how Matterweil or Copra treated you? "

"Your point being?"

"No particular point," said Moscowitz, "at this time."

Michael suddenly noticed that Andre was standing nearby. How long had he been there?

"You will never see me again, Mr. Levine," said Andre. "People in the building have bad thoughts about me, and I cannot live knowing this."

Michael was alarmed. Andre cannot live knowing this?

"Andre, before you do something rash, may I suggest counseling"

"I don't need counseling to quit this madhouse. How many more bodies am I going to find? How much longer must I put up with the way people whisper about me?"

"I always believed in you," said Michael.

"Big fucking deal."

"Andre, I never heard you curse like this before."

"It is the building cursing, not me. I am leaving now, while people are now blaming Calvin. Thank you for promising to clear my name."

Andre Castellano turned and walked out the door into the street.

"What do you want," Moscowitz barked at the EMS worker.

"If we stay here much longer," said the paramedic, "we're going to miss our dinner break."

"And?"

"We'd rather not. It seems like you folks have done everything with the body that you can. We'd like to do our part, and get it the hell out of here."

"And then have dinner?"

"Actually we thought we'd grab a bite on the way."

"Let's do it this way," said Moscowitz. "You take the body to the morgue, and then do whatever you're supposed to after that."

"Sounds good to me," said the paramedic, who raised his right hand in a let's-head-'em-up-and-move-'em-out gesture.

The two EMS workers placed Blanche's corpse, still encased in the trash bag, onto a stretcher. They secured two broad khaki straps around the hidden body. Each took an end of the stretcher, and they started to carry it out.

"I forgot to tell you something," said one stretcher-bearer. "My video store actually has a Fellini flick in stock, *The Clowns*."

"No kidding," said the other. "I've heard of that one; but I've never seen it. I've always liked Fellini. I never saw this one. Is it any good?"

"Oh yes," said the first. "It was made as a television documentary; but it's got a lot of depth."

Moscowitz, Michael and Tatum watched the two carry the stretcher out.

"Tatum," said Moscowitz, "in addition to looking for signs of blood in the hallways, have the uniforms knock on every door, and find out if anybody heard something, saw something, smelled something, anything."

"We're doing it," said Tatum.

"I don't understand this building," Moscowitz said to Michael. "You've had two murders in the space of a week.

One victim is hacked into pieces, and the other is pounded into hamburger. But nobody heard anything."

"The walls of this building are pretty solid," said Michael. "It gives a lot of privacy. They don't make them like this anymore."

"Oh that's right," said Moscowitz, "you're the new president. Are you out of your mind?"

Michael recalled the image of Blanche Copra's bludgeoned face. Moscowitz walked toward the lobby door, leading to the street, and Michael followed.

"What should I do?" asked Michael.

"If I were you," said Moscowitz, "I wouldn't trust a single one of my neighbors."

"That's no way to live."

"Perhaps," said Moscowitz.

As Michael, trailing Moscowitz, crossed the building's threshold and stepped on the sidewalk, he realized that the police had been joined by local television station crews and newspaper reporters. Moscowitz sliced through them, repeating "nothing to report right now" as he moved.

"Hey," said one of the reporters who pointed at Michael, "that guy's the new president."

As the small crowd of people bearing pens, tape recorders and cameras bobbed toward him, Michael began to truly explore his feelings of fright.

SIXTEEN

A Sudden Chill

"Thank you, Steve," said the blonde television reporter, planted in the middle of Michael's television screen. "A brutal murderer struck again at Olmsted Court, a luxury co-op in Brooklyn. The victim, Blanche Copra – 53 years old – was bludgeoned to death."

The screen showed the two EMS workers wheeling the stretcher bearing Blanche's remains. Their somber demeanor convinced Michael they were talking about Ingmar Bergman.

"She was the co-op's president," continued the reporter, once again onscreen, "and, in fact, was elected to that office only this week, replacing Herman Matterweil, also a murder victim. Neighbors are stunned."

The screen suddenly revealed Mrs. Buxbaum, obviously a stunned neighbor.

"She was a nice lady," said Mrs. Buxbaum, "she never bothered anybody."

"Are you frightened?" asked the reporter.

"Not any more than usual. You live in the city. You get used to it."

Michael suddenly saw himself on the screen. His hair was uncombed and his slacks were too baggy, and he needed a shave.

"I'm talking to Michael Levine, the co-op's new president," said the reporter. "Mr. Levine how do you feel about all this?"

"Troubled," said the Michael on television. "Blanche Copra was very important to us. We'll miss her."

"Are you scared? You might be the next victim."

"I'm aware of that," said Michael. "I try not to think about it. I'm just going to do my job, and have confidence that the police will do theirs."

The camera went back to the reporter.

"So far," she said, "the police have no suspects and few leads. I am told they do want to bring one man in for questioning. He and Ms. Copra argued this afternoon; but currently he is not considered a suspect. Over to you, Steve."

"Thank you, Marie. What kind of hemlines does the high fashion world predict for our pets? We'll have that in a—"

Michael turned the television set off in disgust.

Why did she have to ask if I'm scared, he thought. That's not a question you ask a person who's in the position I'm in. I should have challenged her on that. I should have refused to answer. Who knows what she would have done if I refused to answer? What do I mean by "a person who's in the position I'm in?" I mean I'm a sitting duck.

The phone rang.

"Hello?"

"Mr. Levine?"

"Yes."

"Mr. Michael Levine of Olmsted Court?"

"Yes."

"You don't know me, sir, but I saw you on television just now."

The man on the other end spoke very evenly with just a trace of subdued intensity.

"I have been studying the murder case," the voice continued, "and I have some information that might be of use to you. Do you want to hear it?"

"Please go on," said Michael, reaching for a pen.

"First, Mr. Matterweil was murdered, and if I'm not mistaken, the man was Jewish."

Uh oh, thought Michael.

"I asked myself," said the voice, "why the Zionist dominated media would devote so much attention to the murder of a Jew? That's the kind of thing they like to cover up, you know. Then, Miss Copra was murdered, and I understood."

"What did you understand," Michael found himself asking.

"The complexity of the scheme is beautiful," said the voice in that same determined tone. "She was Christian. The Zionist conspirators are tired of Jews being executed for their crimes. So they kill one of their own, then they kill an American. Then they'll kill one of their own again, of course. That's you. Then they'll kill an American. They'll kill one of their own. They'll kill—"

Michael hung up in mid-kill.

The phone rang. Michael slowly stuck his hand out, picked up the phone and placed the receiver next to his ear.

"Mr. Levine, obviously you cannot stand the truth."

It was the voice, and Michael hung up.

The phone rang again. Michael didn't move. The phone continued to ring, and Michael started counting the rings. By the thirteenth, he couldn't control himself any longer. He picked up the phone, and snarled into the mouthpiece, "Look you, if you don't stop bothering me, I'll get the cops after your ass."

"Why Michael," said Dolores, "what a sweet thing to say."

"Oh God!"

The story of Michael's meeting tumbled out of his lips. The nonstop stream of the murder, his presidency, the television news, and those awful phone calls poured forth.

"I don't know what I'll do about the phone," said Michael. "I can't unplug it because my patients need me. I don't want to deal with that guy or anybody else like him on the phone."

"Use your answering machine," said Dolores.

"Oh, that's a good idea. He called me because he saw me on television. Isn't that weird? Being on television was strange."

"I saw it," said Dolores. You poor dear."

"I'm so glad you called, Dolores. I wanted to call you earlier."

"Why didn't you?"

"I didn't want to bother you because I know you're working."

"You're learning. That's good."

"I wanted to call you when I returned home this afternoon just to tell you that I think you're wonderful and that I adore you."

"That might have been permissible," said Dolores.

"Then, there was the murder and the presidency. Did I tell you I'm president of the co-op?"

"Yes, and I heard it on television," said Dolores.

"I'm very nervous. That lady on television was right. I might get killed. I have lunatics who don't know me, explaining why I'll be murdered. Sergeant Moscowitz asked me if I'm crazy."

"Why don't you resign?"

"I can't. I know this sounds stupid; but I'm needed. If the cooperative falls apart, so many lives will be affected. It's my chance to do something for somebody else, even if it – well, it's my chance to do something."

"Even if it kills you?"

"I'll be all right."

"If you insist on being president," said Dolores, "make sure you double-lock your doors."

"I will."

"And, say your prayers."

"I promise."

"And don't forget to floss."

"Now, wait a minute."

"I've got to go now, Michael; but I've been thinking about you all day. I'm going to dream about you tonight."

"Oh God," said Michael. "Goodnight Dolores."

"Good night, Michael."

Michael woke up the next morning at 5:47. That's when the first phone call came in. Happily, it was not last night's crank. Unhappily, it was a shareholder wondering where the hell the hot water was. Michael had not realized until that moment that the burdens of the presidency included explaining the absence of hot water to a person in search of a morning shower.

"I'll call the super right away," said Michael, "and set him straight."

"You better make that long distance," said the caller. "I understand he fled to North Carolina."

"Oh that's right," said Michael. "Calvin disappeared yesterday."

The phone rang at two-minute intervals. Michael quickly learned to let the answering machine handle the calls.

A few minutes before nine Walter dropped off a bundle of assorted papers for Michael to review. These included invoices, letters from lawyers, contracts for various services, and other assorted financial records.

"Did you get many phone calls about the hot water problem?" asked Michael.

"What hot water problem?" asked Walter.

"There's no hot water this morning," said Michael.

"No kidding," said Walter. "I took a shower about 20 minutes ago and there was plenty of hot water."

"What about Calvin?"

"What about Calvin?"

"Doesn't he have to turn the hot water on?"

"He has to know how to turn it on, but I think it works automatically."

"Oh," said Michael.

After his morning coffee, Michael began to study the pieces of paper. He intended to learn all the boring Olmsted Court details. He remembered something he learned about Lincoln. The martyred president was unhappy with how his generals were proceeding in the Civil War. Therefore Lincoln taught himself military strategy. The image of Lincoln trailing his big, bony fingers across maps blended with the schoolboy Lincoln studying by the light of the hearth.

Michael examined the documents with numbers sprayed across them like pox, and likened himself to Lincoln. Both were presidents in time of crisis. If old Honest Abe could learn about the movements of armies and supply lines, thought Michael, then I should conquer the mystique of bookkeeping.

At first, he thought he would divide the invoices into "paid" and "unpaid" piles. He soon realized the invoices already were separated that way. Then, he decided to divide them according to the type of contracting work they covered. He succeeded in blanketing the table with five orderly piles.

Now what, he wondered. Just what am I looking for? Good question. I'm not looking for anything in particular. I want to absorb this information. I want to get a profile of this building. I want to go home.

Michael erased the Lincolnesque image, and instead thought of himself as a history student. He was poring over arcane documents that would yield clues about that strange tribe, known as Olmsted Courters. He learned little about the culture except that it owed $40,000 to Wel-Dunne Contractors, the firm that did all the building's repairs. That's a lot of money to owe a contractor, Michael thought.

He wanted to learn about the Wel-Dunne debt from Walter. He still didn't know Walter's work number. Michael thought he might have received it some time before and that it was scrawled across some piece of paper in his files. His own Olmsted Court files were planted in a cardboard carton in his office. He slowly removed the file folder labeled "Board," and methodically riffled through the papers.

The phone number wasn't there. He studied contents of another file folder, "contacts," and the phone number wasn't there. He placed the second folder on top of the first. Soon, he was racing through his files and created a teetering pile of folders. No phone number for Walter. The only folder that remained in the carton was labeled "Pre-co-oping."

I'll call Ethel, he decided. She'll have his number.

As he reached for the telephone, his left elbow grazed the heap of folders, and propelled them toward the floor. Upon impact, pieces of paper tumbled out of the folders, and Michael could see his files scattered on the floor.

I really hope Ethel has the number, he thought.

Michael counted 20 rings before he concluded Ethel wasn't in. After hanging up, he kept his hand on the receiver, as if to coax some hint from the instrument. He stared at the Wel-Dunne invoices, and at his scrambled files. Wistfully, Michael decided he could do no more at this point, and placed the papers Walter had brought back into their envelope.

Michael gazed dumbly at the 9x12 envelope, and dispassionately noted a company logo in the left-hand corner.

Wait a minute, thought Michael, that's where Walter works. I could call that company and speak to Walter and learn whatever it is I want to know. Research is so important.

"Oh yes," said Walter, "those guys have saved our lives. They've got plumbers, electricians, plasterers. Herman brought them in early on. I don't know where he found them; but they've done service above and beyond."

"No kidding," said Michael.

"You should know this," said Walter, "you're on the Board."

"There are some details I never paid attention to," admitted Michael.

"I guess that's okay, as long as other people are paying attention," said Walter charitably. "Anyway, a lot of work had to be done quickly, and our payables with them were in a real mess. Herman worked out a deal, though, where, regardless of the work done that month, we made regular payments of $12,000 a month."

"Is that usual?" asked Michael.

"I don't think so. I suspect Herman's very — Herman was very shrewd and persuasive. Herman was able to get them to lower their hourly rates. They charge us less per hour than the contractors we first used, and for that matter less than any we've contacted."

"No kidding," said Michael, "so our repair bills are lower."

"Not exactly," said Walter. "These guys seem to be more thorough, so they take more time. They come whenever we call them and emergencies have a knack of taking place after hours. Overtime often is called for. But Herman worked out a good deal and they never beat us over the head for the money."

"Oh boy," said Michael. "They must have heard about Herman's death by now. I better call them and let them know we'd like to continue with them. Could I have their number please?"

"Sure."

Walter made tongue-clicking sounds as he thumbed through his address book.

"This is strange," said Walter, "I don't have a phone number for them – just a post office box. Not so strange, I guess. Herman is the one who dealt with them. Calvin would have the phone number."

"Calvin is on the lam," said Michael.

"What a shame we have to lose him," said Walter. "He's really a good super. You know, he's another reason our repair system was so good. A shareholder would report a problem. Calvin would come in, poke around, do some tests, and often he was able to discover the real source of the problem was far more serious than initially suspected. Who knows how many emergencies he prevented?"

"Let me have the post office box," said Michael.

"Oh sure. It's PO Box 2191, Adelphi Station, Brooklyn NY 11238. Are you going to call the post office?"

"They wouldn't tell me; but I have to find some way to contact them. If worse comes to worst, I'll send them a letter."

"Okay," said Walter, "so long."

"Bye-bye," said Michael.

Hanging up, Michael wondered once again why he could have a perfectly reasonable adult conversation and end it like a toddler by saying "bye-bye."

Michael removed the "Pre-cooping" folder from the carton. An imp of an urge whispered that he should toss it on the floor with the rest of the files. Instead, he aimlessly leafed through the contents — lawyers' letters, ad hoc committee declarations of one sort or another. Michael felt nostalgic.

From this crazy energy, he thought, came our co-op.

As Michael read one of Herman Matterweil's letters, he felt a sudden chill.

"This will be a cooperative," wrote Matterweil, "and we need everybody's cooperation. If you have some interest in being part of this wonderful enterprise; but some personal consideration impedes your participation, contact me. If you are anxious to do so with maximum discretion, you needn't visit or phone me. Just send a letter to my post office box. That's Box 2191, Adelphi Station, Brooklyn NY 11238."

Michael thought about his eulogy for Herman. Yes, thought Michael, Herman left us many gifts – pride, dignity and Wel-Dunne Contractors.

SEVENTEEN

Getting a Bit Testy

Maybe Moscowitz is in the building, thought Michael. He rushed down to the lobby.

"Mr. Levine," said Archie, "I got to talk to you."

"In a minute, Archie. Is Sergeant Moscowitz around?"

"Yes, but there's a matter of importance I have to take up with you."

"In a minute, Archie. Where is Moscowitz?"

"It's about this crazy girl that sees you. The one with the mouth. Marjorie."

"I'm really interested in looking for Moscowitz."

"Yeah, I know. So I took her out last night."

Michael wondered if it were against professional ethics for a therapist's doorman to have a relationship with a patient.

"She seemed kind of cute," said Archie, "And I got the idea that she took a shine to me. A lot of girls go for the uniform. I thought she was just weird enough to want a few kicks. We were having a nice time when all of a sudden, she starts with that mouth of hers. She got very nasty, and I found myself screaming at her."

"Archie, I don't think you should be telling me this."

"Well, the thing is, if she tells you that I was abusive to her, make sure she tells you the whole story."

"Archie, this isn't right. I can't discuss my patients with you."

"I just want to get the record straight. Nobody's asking me; but I know exactly what's wrong with that girl."

"Oh, really, and what is that?"

"She's off her rocker. She is one crazy chick."

"Thanks for the second opinion. Where's Sergeant Moscowitz?"

"In Mr. Matterweil's apartment."

Officer Tatum admitted Michael to the apartment. Moscowitz sat in Herman's easy chair and read the *New York Times*. He carefully folded the paper and put it aside.

Michael dutifully told the story of looking through the invoices, his conversation with Walter, and his subsequent discovery that Wel-Dunne's box number apparently belonged to Herman Matterweil.

"It was a scam," said Michael in disbelief. "Calvin Birmingham had to be in on it. I'm remembering all the times that I would complain about something in my apartment and Calvin would come marching in, look at the problem, get up on a ladder, get down on his knees, press the wall gingerly, and look very serious. He calls the contractors, and they come in like the cavalry.

"The shareholder sees what looks like a lot of work going on in the apartment, and feels fortunate. Herman racks up the dollars and Birmingham gets his cut for his part."

"Very good," said Moscowitz, "very neat and sound theorizing. So who's the killer?"

"Well," said Michael, "Blanche Copra and Calvin Birmingham had that argument about repairs. Maybe he expected her to join in on the scheme. She refused, and he realized she was going to put a big dent in his income. Furthermore she humiliated him by yelling at him in public. So he killed her."

"What about Matterweil?"

"What?"

"If Matterweil was the goose that lay the golden egg for Birmingham, why would Birmingham kill him?"

"Good question," said Michael. "I don't know."

"Maybe," said Moscowitz, "Birmingham wanted a bigger cut."

"Right," said Michael, "that could be it."

"Or perhaps Matterweil was going to fire Birmingham."

"That's possible," said Michael.

"Or it could be," said Moscowitz, "that the two men had a more intimate relationship, and it went sour."

"Do you really think so?" asked Michael. "Nahhh. Really?"

"It's a possibility."

"I suppose."

"Or maybe there are two murderers."

"Two murderers?"

"Sure. One person had a grudge against Matterweil, and cut him into little pieces. And along comes Copra and this other fine citizen says, 'That's a good idea.'"

"Two murderers?"

"Sure. At first glance, the two homicides seem to reflect two different styles. Matterweil was carved up, and

Copra was bludgeoned. The first seems to have been planned, premeditated. The second was sudden and explosive. There's also a sexual overtone to the second murder that seems to be absent in the first.

"Finally," continued Moscowitz, "my educated guess is that if you have only a single homicidal maniac running around here, then Calvin Birmingham is off the hook. He seems to have had absolutely no motive for the Matterweil killing."

"What about those possibilities you mentioned before?" asked Michael.

"They still stand as possibilities, and I still have to explore them."

"Do you think Birmingham did kill Blanche?" Michael asked.

"He certainly had a motive," said Moscowitz, "She cut his balls off in public. Some guys don't like that.

"As for opportunity, I suspect he would have ample opportunity. He knows the building inside and out. He knows when people come and go, and where they are. We don't have the murder weapon and, at this point, we can't reconstruct the actual steps and details of either crime.

"And," continued Moscowitz, "We can't restrict our investigation only to people who live in Olmsted Court."

"True," said Michael, "Very true."

"It could be one of your patients, for example."

"No," said Michael. "No way."

"And why is that unthinkable?"

"Because my patients don't kill people."

"I'd like a list of your patients."

"I can't do that. That would be an invasion of their privacy."

"So?"

"I can't do that."

"I can make you do it. It will take a while; but I'll get my way. I'd rather do it sooner than later, so I'd like your cooperation."

"No."

Moscowitz smiled and Michael felt a chill.

The phone rang. Moscowitz nodded to Tatum who then picked up the receiver.

"Yeah," said Tatum.

Moscowitz stared intently at the police officer, who alternately doodled and grunted. Michael felt obliged to stare, in turn, at Moscowitz. As Tatum hung up, he clenched his left fist and pointed the thumb upwards.

"It's a go," he said.

"Then, let's do it," said Moscowitz.

"Do what?" asked Michael.

"We just obtained a court order to review and remove Blanche Copra's effects. Apparently, her two surviving sisters wanted to divvy up the stuff, and felt that something as time-consuming as a murder investigation would mess with their ability to increase their material holdings. There is a ray of sunshine for you."

"What's that?"

"There will be no funeral. They're just going to fry her in a crematorium with no ceremony and then fight over her ashes. Probably, the loser gets the ashes."

"So," said Michael, "you weren't just hanging out and reading the paper. You were waiting for that court order."

"Very astute of you," said Moscowitz.

"And you're going to go through all of her possessions to see if there's a clue, or to find some item that links up with something in the Matterweil effects."

"Very good," said Moscowitz. "We'll make a cop out of you yet."

Moscowitz and Tatum moved toward Matterweil's front door.

"I guess this means you don't need my list of patients," said Michael.

The sharp crash of the door that slammed behind the two policemen informed Michael that he was in Herman's apartment by himself.

The door opened, and Moscowitz stuck his head back into the apartment.

"Of course we do," he said.

The door slammed again.

EIGHTEEN

No Offense Taken

Michael quickly left Herman's apartment and headed for the lobby. As the elevator door creaked open, Michael saw Millicent Martin standing defensively in the corner. Her clenched teeth held a khaki athletic whistle, tied to a red ribbon that hung around her neck. Her right hand, at shoulder level, tightly gripped a small can of mace. Her puffed-up cheeks suggested she was just about to blow into the whistle.

"It's only me, Dr. Martin," said Michael.

She blinked in recognition and her cheeks slowly lost their deposit of air; but her mace-bearing right hand remained poised.

"I believe," she said, "in taking as few chances as possible."

"I guess that makes sense," said Michael.

"You ought to know," she said.

The five shareholders waiting for the elevator in the lobby gave Michael plenty of room as he got out. A police officer, stationed in the building, stood near Archie's post. The elevator door started to close but none of the lingering quintet wanted to travel with any of the others.

"Come on," said Michael, "you've known each other for years."

"We've probably known the murderer for years, too," said Krane.

Panic crossed Roberta Haven's face.

"There are five of you," said Michael. "Don't forget safety in numbers."

"You should talk," said Krane, the last one to enter the elevator. "You're already a dead man. Meaning no offense."

"No offense taken," muttered Michael

"Don't just stand there," shrieked Evelyn Ross. "Help me with my packages."

Evelyn Ross was shouting at the policeman. Archie held the front door open, while Evelyn Ross alternately pointed at her department store boxes piled on the curb and the dark blue tie hanging from the policeman's neck.

"I-I don't—" stammered the policeman.

"You're here to help, aren't you?"

"Well, yes."

"I'm here to be helped."

"I'm not supposed to give that kind of help."

Evelyn Ross glared at the policeman.

"I don't carry packages," said the cop resentfully. "I fight crime."

"Archie," barked Mrs. Ross, "the packages."

Michael found his voice.

"Evelyn," he said. "Archie has to watch the door."

"You watch the door. Archie, step lively."

Archie walked to the curb. He squeezed two packages under his left arm; insinuated one package under his right arm; and gripped each of the remaining two department store boxes in his hands. He swaggered toward the front door which Michael opened for him.

"Just bring them in like a good fellow," said Evelyn Ross, "and I'll take it from there."

Archie placed the boxes in front of the elevator carefully, as if he were assembling Stonehenge. Evelyn Ross reached into her purse, and thrust a crumpled dollar bill into Archie's right hand.

"Something for your trouble," she said.

"Oh, Mrs. Ross, you shouldn't have," replied Archie, while sticking the dollar into his back pocket.

"I'm sorry," Michael told the policeman, while Archie returned to his station.

"I'm not here to carry packages," said the policeman. "I fight crime."

"That's exactly what you told her," said Michael. "And you were right."

"I know hand-to-hand combat."

"That's very interesting," said Michael. "It must be tough."

"It's a science," said the cop. "You've got to get them in the crotch before they get you. It isn't just the hand-to-hand combat. I know CPR. I'm trained to ascertain any suspicious situation. I can quell a riot with the best of them. I'm not supposed to carry packages."

"I understand" said Michael.

"I'm a trained professional," said the policeman.

"And a good one, too, I'm sure," said Michael.

The elevator door opened at the lobby level, and a screaming Donna Kurland leapt out, knocking aside Evelyn Ross's packages.

"It's terrible," wailed Donna Kurland.

"Oh no," said Michael. "Not again."

"I just got a horrible leak in my apartment!" screamed Kurland. "My wallpaper, my tile floor, my tennis rackets, they're all ruined."

Her running shoes indeed were saturated, and there was a trail of tread patterns along the lobby's terrazzo floor.

"Get the super," Donna Kurland demanded.

"We have a little problem in that area," said Michael.

"My wallpaper never had a chance," she said. "It was backordered and took five months to arrive. What are you going to do?"

"Archie," said Michael, "there's a handyman on now, isn't there?"

"Willie's on," said Archie, "but I don't know what he's on. Better to call the plumber."

"Right! Still, tell Willie to turn off the water in the C-line. We have to get a plumber. I don't want to use Wel-Dunne. We have to find another plumber."

"I have the phone number," said Archie, "of the guy we used to use."

"We'll get this under control," Michael said. "We've got this under control."

Over Donna Kurland's shoulder Michael could see Evelyn Ross approaching. Great flames roared in her large eyes.

"You knocked over my packages," Evelyn told Donna.

"It was an emergency," said Donna, "and they were in my way."

"They are my boxes," said Evelyn Ross. "They contain precious things. They were not intended to be knocked about by your big klutzy feet."

"Klutzy feet," repeated Donna Kurland. "I'll kick your ass with my klutzy feet."

"Excuse me, ladies," said Michael.

"Shut up," said Donna Kurland.

"Shut up," said Evelyn Ross.

"You both have hurt feelings." Said Michael, "but maybe we can examine what's going on, and—"

"He never, ever shuts up," said Donna Kurland.

"Just yak, yak, yak," said Evelyn Ross.

"This is almost as dangerous as a drug bust," said the policeman.

"Tell me about it," said Archie. "If they gave medals to doormen, I'd be too weighted down to walk."

"Archie," said Michael, "please get Willie and the plumber. I just remembered an appointment."

"Look at him run out," said Evelyn Ross.

"But I have a luncheon appointment," Michael lied.

"You mean like in the condemned man ate a hearty meal?" asked Donna Kurland.

Everyone but Michael snickered. He was already in the street and on his way to the movies.

The bright greens and cheerful flowers in the florist shop two doors away from the Cineplex made Michael think of Dolores. His smile widened into a grin as he entered the shop and saw lilies, orchids, chrysanthemums, tulips, purples, whites, tropical dazzlers, red, white, yellow roses. No question about it. He would send her a dozen roses. Before, during and after the film, Michael called Dolores. He left a message each of the first two times that her answering machine picked up. But on the third call, he hung up without leaving a message, and took a cab home.

NINETEEN

Visit Hawaii

Moscowitz studied the "Visit Hawaii" poster taped to the glass partition of his office. It depicted a bright moonlit beach with hula dancers swaying on white sands. The sergeant hoped to be on that beach some day. Tatum disturbed his reverie with a discernible whoop.

Moscowitz looked up.

Everyone in the office froze and looked up.

"It's whacko time," Tatum shouted. "Come on everybody, let's do the whacko."

Moscowitz, along with others, approached slowly, gently, not wishing to agitate the man by any sudden movements. Tatum faced a long wooden worktable on which were piled many boxes of material removed from Matterweil's apartment. He flashed a wide grin. Moscowitz had been looking forward to that smile.

"What have you got?" Moscowitz asked.

"Whackos."

Tatum held aloft an accordion-pleated manila folder.

"Herman Matterweil," said Tatum, "put all the corre-spondence that annoyed him into this folder which he labeled 'The Whacko File.' It was in the bottom of one of the boxes."

Moscowitz pawed the thick folder and grabbed heaps of paper. An abundance of daggers, nooses, and skull-and-crossbones-decorated bottles adorned the folder. Mos-cowitz flipped through the neatly typed entreaties on lush letterheads, the demands on spiral notebook lined paper, the pleas, the suggestions, the complaints. They asked for repairs, offered explanations for late payments, and told of rules that should be eliminated or added.

Moscowitz felt as if he were kicked in the stomach by something else that he saw. Matterweil wrote nasty comments across the letters. In the privacy of his own apartment the grown-up, stuffy Matterweil was gone. In-stead, a thumb-nosing 67-year-old, sleazy brat wrote things like "Fat Chance" and "Go to Hell, Ha Ha Ha" across the letters. One scrawled, unsigned note pleaded, "Please leave lovers alone." On this, Matterweil drew carefully-labeled immature figures engaging in sexual acts and added the notation, "Thurs. 10 p.m."

"Herman," began a letter from Krane the salesman, "you stole my company from me and I won't forget it."

"It looks," said Moscowitz, "like we have to start 'Operation Whacko.'"

TWENTY

How's That For Reality?

"Oh, this place," said the driver as his taxicab jerked to a stop in front of Olmsted Court. "Ain't this the horror house?"

"That's what one paper calls it," said Michael, "but trust me, this really is a great building."

"Right," said the driver, "so who's the next to get iced?"

"You and your mother," mumbled Michael as he slammed the door.

Stomping into the lobby, Michael mentally relived the semi-encounter with the cabdriver, and he barely heard Archie.

"Your new honey is here."

"My new what?"

"Me," said Dolores. "He's talking about me."

Dolores. It was Dolores. She was dressed simply in old, faded jeans that looked so soft on her body and a tailored chambray work shirt that hugged her braless breasts. Her blonde hair was tied behind her head, and small rhinestone earrings caught the light. A large purple nylon pouch hung from her shoulder. Michael had to kiss her.

When their lips finally parted, Michael stared at Dolores and beamed.

"I loved the roses, Michael," she said.

"Oh, you got them?"

"I had just the perfect vase for them."

"And they brought you over here?"

"I've been hearing about the murders on the news," said Dolores, "and I just didn't think you should be alone."

Michael squeezed Dolores's hands.

"I'm sorry for the trouble Archie gave you," said Michael.

"Archie?"

"The doorman," said Michael.

"Oh, he didn't give me any trouble," said Dolores. "He's kind of cute."

"Cute? Archie cute?"

At the door leading to his apartment, Michael hesitated before he placed the key into the lock, and then opened the door, walked into the foyer, and turned on the light. Dolores followed. It was an historic moment that called for coffee.

Michael disappeared into the kitchen, and Dolores sat in his living room wingback chair. Three pre-World War I photographs in matching pewter frames caught her eye. The pictures (a man, a woman, and the two together) hung as a set on the wall near the window. The plump-faced woman in the photo pressed her lips tightly together. She wore a dark high-necked dress, and her hair was piled tightly atop her head. The man had close-cropped hair, a thick mustache, and a determined expression. A pocket-watch chain arced across the vest of his three-piece suit.

"I see you're admiring my family," said Michael, as he entered the room with a tray full of coffee paraphernalia. He set the tray on the chrome and glass table that sat in front of the steel gray couch. Michael settled into a corner of the couch.

"I love that kind of photograph," said Dolores as she moved over to the other end of the couch. "Are they your grandparents?"

"I don't think so," said Michael. "I found them in a second-hand store over in Park Slope. Sometimes I tell people it's my family. The camera never lies but beware the owner of the pictures."

"Right," said Dolores. "Have you ever seen the photo of JFK in the Oval Office? His back is to us. His head is down. His arms are outspread. Clearly it documents the burdens of the presidency."

"Yes," said Michael. "It's a powerful, powerful picture."

"It is," said Dolores, "and there's one little interesting detail. Kennedy's arms were stretched out, and his head was down because he was reading a newspaper, the *Herald Tribune.* He was annoyed and amused by what he was reading. 'Where do they get this stuff?' he asked the photographer. How's that for reality?"

"I'll show you reality," Michael said.

He leaned over and kissed Dolores on the lips. Gradually, he eased his mouth down to her neck and presented her with a few more kisses.

Dolores placed her right hand on Michael's cheek. Michael closed his eyes in pleasant expectation. Her fingertips trailed down to the front of his shirt. She grabbed a handful of his shirt and tugged. Michael followed the gravitational pull until he was exceedingly next to Dolores.

"Oh, Dolores, you smell so good."

She unbuttoned his shirt. With each released button, she planted a kiss upon his chest. His hands moved to her shirt and stroked the contours.

The telephone rang, and Michael froze. The phone rang again, and then a third time.

On the fourth ring, his answering machine took over.

"Hello, this is Michael Levine. I'm sorry I'm not available to take your call; but at the machine's beep, please leave your name, phone number, day and time of calling and any message. Take as long as you like."

"Mr. Levine, this is Calvin. Calvin Birmingham. I can't leave my phone number. I believe you know why. There was trouble with the boiler today so I personally had to get the hot water going. I can't guarantee that I can do it tomorrow. I believe you know why. I believe you ought to hire a temporary super. Call my brother-in-law, Albert. He's a good man. Archie's got his number."

There was a click.

"I should call the police," said Michael.

"What will you tell them?" asked Dolores.

"They're looking for him," Michael explained. "I'll tell them that Calvin called, and the message he left, and I guess I'll give them the answering machine cassette."

Michael slowly removed himself from the couch, and walked toward the kitchen. Dolores brought her legs onto the couch and rearranged herself into a curl.

Michael returned and sat beside her.

"I left a message for him to call me."

"Maybe I should check my machine," said Dolores who disappeared into the kitchen

She tumbled onto the couch when she returned.

"There were two messages from you, my poor lost man," she said.

"I really had to see you," said Michael.

"Also, some jerk called and didn't leave a message," she said. "That really steams me."

"I know what you mean," said Michael, "It's so damned inconsiderate."

"No other calls," said Dolores, "so it looks like we have some free time."

Michael and Dolores clung together in silence. Their hands started to move along each other's body. They touched and marveled and sighed.

Dolores unbuttoned her blouse.

"You are so beautiful," whispered Michael.

He took her hand and led her toward his bedroom. Suddenly, he stopped in the doorway.

"Dolores," said Michael, "I can't stand it. That was me on the phone. I was the one who didn't leave a message. Forgive me?"

TWENTY-ONE

Oh, the Pickles

A sudden puff of air tickled Michael into wakefulness. Dolores, dressed only in her chambray work shirt, was covering Michael with a sheet. The edge of the thin cloth trailed across Michael's chest, and he truly felt loved.

As he closed his eyes, Michael could hear her padding out of the room. He was fairly certain that he was awake; but he had no desire to remove himself from the couch. Dolores was in the kitchen, a fact verified by the sound of running water, and the occasional chiming of kitchenware. Aromas of coffee and slowly sizzling butter slipped into Michael's nostrils.

When Michael opened his eyes Dolores was arranging the carafe of coffee, two mugs, a milk pitcher, a platter of French toast, two plates, knives and forks, napkins, and a bottle of Camp's pure maple syrup.

"French toast," said Michael gratefully. "You made French toast. Is it Saturday morning?"

"No," said Dolores, "it's just Thursday evening."

Michael sat up.

Dolores placed two pieces of French toast on Michael's plate, and nudged the plate toward him. She poured coffee into a mug, and also passed that over to him. She then served herself, and sat cross-legged on the floor. Michael slipped down to the floor to join her. He poured syrup across his toast. He cut the toast into little pieces and then poked his fork through the largest piece, which he promptly delivered to his mouth.

"Oh this is good," said Michael.

"But of course," said Dolores.

"The thing that amazes me the most," said Michael.

"Yes?"

"The maple syrup! I've been searching for that for months. I knew I had some. I just didn't know where it was."

"It was in your refrigerator," said Dolores.

"That much I had guessed."

"It was on the top shelf, in the back, behind the large jar of pickles."

"Oh, the pickles," said Michael. "I bought them because they were on sale, and it seemed like a good idea to have pickles in the house. I just never got around to having any. I guess I just didn't see the pickles when I looked, so the jar became a wall and anything behind it was rendered invisible."

"I'm glad we got to the bottom of that," said Dolores.

Michael reached for the last piece of French toast on the platter. Dolores blocked his move with the artful thrust of her fork.

"Nuh-uh-uh," she said. "That one is mine."

"I thought you were finished," said Michael.

"Lame excuse," she said. "You didn't think at all. You just wanted what you wanted."

"What I really want is you," said Michael, reaching under her shirt.

"Not while we're fighting over French toast."

"What's your problem?"

"It's not my problem, doctor. It's yours."

"So what's going on, here?" asked Michael. "Is this – Are we--?"

"Putting an end to all this? Not just yet."

"I wasn't even that hungry," said Michael. "It just tasted so good."

"Sweet talk won't help you here," said Dolores.

"I'm sorry?"

"Are you telling me or asking me?"

"I'm telling you," said Michael. "I'm sorry. I am sorry. I had my share. I should have at least asked."

"Better," said Dolores.

She delicately lifted the remaining, once disputed slice of French toast, and eased it onto her plate. Michael watched admiringly as she cut each piece, lifted it to her mouth, slowly chewed and swallowed. When she finished, she demurely dabbed at her mouth with a napkin, and groped for Michael.

Thursday evening was good. Michael and Dolores slowly moved their choreography from living room to bathroom shower to bedroom. They returned to the living room at eleven for dinner which thoughtfully had been delivered to the door by a Flatbush Avenue Chinese restaurant. The two greedily gobbled up steamed dumplings, hot and sour soup, tofu Szechwan style, and eggplant in garlic sauce.

"Would you like some more tofu?" Michael asked.

"No, thank you," said Dolores.

"May I finish it?"

"Yes, you may."

After clearing away the dinner debris, Dolores and Michael watched television in the living room. She sat on the right hand side of the couch. He lay across the couch with his head safely cradled in her lap. The remote control switcher rested on the arm of the couch next to Dolores.

"Anything but the news," said Michael.

They enjoyed the PBS pledge drive for a while, and then switched to a *Hill Street Blues* rerun.

"This is not exactly escape fare," said Michael.

"Let's change it."

"No, maybe I'll learn something."

Finally, it was time to retire. Michael switched off all lights, double-locked the door, checked the stove to make sure all burners were fully turned off, and checked sinks and tubs to make sure all faucets were turned off.

Dolores brought her bag into the bedroom. She burrowed through it for her toothbrush and nightie.

In bed, Michael's arm curled around Dolores. As she rolled against him, the fingers of her right hand spread against his chest. The two fell asleep in silent snug security.

It wasn't the ringing telephone that awoke Michael and Dolores at two in the morning. Nor was it the doorbell that shook them out of bed. It had to be the knocking on the door. It had to be the loud, rapid thumping that made Michael jump and nearly knock Dolores out of bed.

As Michael, hastily garbed in an orange robe, was about to unlock the door, Dolores put a restraining hand on his shoulder.

This warning gesture sent *New York Post* headlines dancing through his head. Maybe that sinister someone came knocking at Herman's door and Blanche's door. And then a silly thought took over.

"Mother of God," he said, "is this the end of Little Michael?"

He peered through the door's peephole, and smiled. Mrs. Fazio, and her dog Pom-Pom, stood in the hallway. Michael pulled open the door.

"Oh," said Mrs. Fazio, whose eyes widened at the sight of Dolores, "I didn't know that you had company."

"Um," said Michael, "uh, Dolores, this is Mrs. Fazio. Mrs. Fazio, this is Dolores Caruso."

"Pleased to meet you," said Dolores.

"Likewise, I'm sure," said Mrs. Fazio. "I don't think I've seen you around the neighborhood. Are you new here?"

"I live in Manhattan," said Dolores. "I'm just here for — uh — right now."

"My son has an apartment in Manhattan. In Hell's Kitchen. What do they call that now? Clinton! I'm supposed to call it Clinton. He gets very mad when I call it—"

"Mrs. Fazio," said Michael, "did you have something to tell me?"

"Oh yes! Just a few minutes ago, my little Pom-Pom was barking and barking, and he's such a good dog, so I knew something was wrong. I said, 'What's the matter, Pom-Pom?'

"Pom-Pom just kept on barking," continued Mrs. Fazio. "There was nobody at my door. I checked ever so carefully and there was nobody in the hall. Then, I heard these footsteps. Somebody was on the backstairs. I'll bet you it's the murderer."

"Did you call the police?" asked Michael.

"Oh no," said Mrs. Fazio. "It might be nothing with nothing, and then I would be wasting their time. I thought it would be better if I told you."

"Right," said Michael, "I have all the time in the world."

"That's what I thought," said Mrs. Fazio.

"I'll look into it," said Michael.

"He'll look into it, Pom-Pom," Mrs. Fazio assured the dog.

Back in his bedroom, Michael hurriedly got dressed. He omitted socks as a concession to speed.

"Are you really going to check on this?" asked Dolores.

"You heard the woman," said Michael. "We can't bother the police with this. I'll be all right. I'm taking my baseball bat with me."

"What about the killer?"

"He'll have to get his own baseball bat."

"I'm serious," said Dolores.

"Like she said, it's probably nothing."

"I'm going with you," said Dolores, quickly pulling her jeans on.

"Aren't you going to wear panties?" asked Michael.

"Aren't you going to wear socks?" asked Dolores.

"It's different," said Michael. "Anyway, I don't want you to go. It could be dangerous."

"I've survived civil wars and pitched labor union battles, and terrorists and drug bust shootouts," said Dolores. "Surely I could survive your building?"

"Really," asked Michael, "you did all that stuff?"

"Sure," said Dolores, "all in a day's work. Just give me a baseball bat."

"I only have one."

"Give me a hammer," said Dolores, "give me the frying pan."

"I'll give you a frying pan," said Michael.

Olmsted Court had two staircases. There was the clearly visible main flight of steps. It ran right through the middle of the building and everyone used it. Then, there was the back staircase. Olmsted Courters gained access to these flights by fire doors, one of which was located on each floor.

The incandescent yellow bulbs lighting the backstairs created shadows, one with a baseball bat and the other with a frying pan. Michael stopped at the floor below and picked up a folded, yellowed newspaper crammed into a corner. One headline referred to President Ford. Michael showed the paper to Dolores and then stuck it in his back pocket.

At the next floor, they heard a muffled swishing sound. As they descended, the sound became more defined. It was the bass rhythms of contemporary dance music.

Michael cupped his mouth against Dolores's ear, and whispered, "There is someone down there. I'm going to check. You go back up and call the police."

He handed her the apartment keys. She put her mouth against his ear and whispered, "Be careful!"

He nodded and continued downward, as she went up.

Calvin Birmingham was sitting in the fifth floor stairwell when Michael approached. Birmingham was eating Kentucky Fried Chicken from a Styrofoam plate, and drinking Tropicana orange juice.

"This coleslaw they give you sucks, man," said Birmingham.

"A lot of people are looking for you," said Michael.

"Yeah, I know," said the super. "That Copra bitch. She was a mean bitch; but nobody should have killed her. She wasn't that important."

"Can I sit down?" asked Michael.

"Sure," said Birmingham, "you want some fries?"

"No thanks."

"Hey, what are you doing with that bat? You going to play baseball?"

"No," said Michael. "Somebody told me she heard a noise on the backstairs, so I came to look. If I knew it was you I wouldn't have brought the bat."

"Some people, if they knew it was me, they would've brought a rope."

"I'm sure that's not true," said Michael. "I think you have a lot of friends in this building."

"Not that Copra bitch," said Birmingham; "but I didn't kill her, and I certainly wouldn't hurt Matterweil."

"So, what do you think you'll do now?" asked Michael.

"What can I do? You're calling the police, right?"

"I think it has to be done," said Michael.

"I'm getting tired of hanging around on these stairs, and sneaking around to turn on the hot water and get some food. Did you call my brother-in-law Albert?"

"I didn't get a chance yet," said Michael, "but it was on my list of things to do tomorrow."

"Okay then, let's go downstairs and wait."

Michael held his baseball bat as if it were a walking stick, and followed Birmingham down the stairs.

TWENTY-TWO

The Shock of Cold Water

Michael and Calvin walked down to the lobby. There, the two chatted about North Carolina. Calvin warmly described his home state, dwelling lovingly on the many natural wonders and the simple splendor of the people. Michael fervently avowed his intention to really visit this most distinguished of states. Meanwhile the doorman/porter mopped the terrazzo floor.

Moscowitz arrived first. Two patrol cars, containing uniformed policemen, soon double-parked behind Moscowitz's car. An assortment of vehicles carrying newspaper, television and radio reporters quickly materialized.

As Moscowitz strode into the lobby, the police officers formed a barrier between the front door and the media. Moscowitz wore a green tweed sportcoat; sharply-creased, rust-brown slacks; a bright yellow sportshirt; and cordovan loafers.

"Hello, Calvin," said Sergeant Moscowitz.

"Hello, sir," said Calvin Birmingham.

"I want you to understand," said Moscowitz, "that you are not under arrest. Regardless of what you may have read or heard, or decided for yourself, we are only interested, at this time, in asking you questions to assist us in our investigation."

"I understand," said Birmingham. "I want you to know I have nothing to hide. But these newspapers are making me real nervous. If the mayor wants to throw my butt in jail, nothing you say is going to stop him. I don't care how fair you say you are. You're going to do what they tell you to do."

"I hear you," said Moscowitz, "and I'm not going to feed you any fairy tales. People downtown know I'm mean, and they don't like to mess with me. Still, you've been around too long to not know how things are. So, here's how we're going to work it. I'm going to act like a cop, and try to find out who the real perpetrator is. You're going to have to act like a suspect and make sure your rights are protected. Okay?"

"Yes."

"Good! Let's start right now. You have the right to remain silent. Even though, I am not arresting you, I am reminding you of your Miranda rights. Anything you say can and will be used against you in a court of law. If you cannot afford legal counsel, a lawyer will be appointed to represent you. Do you understand these rights?"

"Yes."

"Okay, then why we don't we go now?"

Moscowitz and Birmingham started toward the front door. Birmingham stopped and turned to Michael.

"I guess I'm not going to be here to take care of the hot water, Mr. Levine."

"That's okay, Calvin," said Michael. "Good luck."

Sergeant Moscowitz and Calvin Birmingham were through the front door and onto the street, where they were flanked by the police officers. The crowd of journalists, unable to get any information from the police, surged into the building and surrounded Michael. Out of the corner of his eye, Michael noticed a blur race out of the elevator, muscle its way through the media, and run onto Eastern Parkway. The blur proved to be Louis Irving.

As the police entourage sped away, Louis shouted, "Don't worry, Calvin, the People are with you."

Michael watched the cars disappear into the early morning mystery. He gazed at the empty streets, the row of buildings with unlit apartments, and the minimal traffic. It occurred to him that he was out on the hostile street, in the darkness, all by himself.

He immediately rushed inside only to be circled by the rampaging herd of journalists. Rather than feel the pain of their trampling hooves, he stood frozen and answered their questions. His mind was on automatic and he felt as if he were witnessing the process rather than experiencing it. Mostly, they wanted to know about his capture of Calvin Birmingham. It mattered not that (a) he had not truly apprehended Birmingham, and (b) Birmingham was not even under arrest.

Q: Were you scared when you came across Birmingham on the staircase?

A: No! I was scared when I was going down the steps; but when I saw that it was Calvin Birmingham, I felt relieved.

Q: Did he put up much of a fight?

A: No! He did offer me some of his French fries.

Q: Can you sleep better now that he's been arrested?

A: He hasn't been arrested. Sergeant Moscowitz only wanted him for questioning.

"Michael Levine," shouted an indignant voice. "I charge you as a traitor to your class."

It was Louis Irving who shared that observation with Michael. The tight circle of reporters parted so that Louis could confront Michael nose-to-nose.

"Not now, Louis," said Michael.

"Oh, excuse me," said Louis, "I'm interfering with your media exposure. We mustn't stand in the way of Michael Levine being on television. Who cares if he does it by stepping on a poor honest working man?"

Louis Irving was a droplet of blood upon the waters, and the gathered reporters went into a shouting frenzy.

"Who are you?"

"Do you live here?"

"Have you been threatened?"

"Are you a friend of the super?"

"Do you think Birmingham's the murderer?"

"What were you just trying to tell Michael Levine?"

"What kind of a man is Birmingham?"

"Did he do it?"

Louis Irving raised his hands for silence. The journalists leaned toward him. The suddenly forgotten Michael slowly backed up until he now was on the periphery of the crowd.

"My name is Louis Irving," Michael heard Louis shout, "and I'm a worker for peace and justice."

Michael, edging softly toward the elevator, happily observed that the press representatives still were intent on Louis.

"I know a raw deal when I see one," declared Louis, "and I can tell you that Calvin Birmingham is being framed because of his race."

The elevator opened and Michael gently stepped inside, pressed a button, watched the doors close, and went home.

Dolores already had returned to bed. She lay, body slightly curled, on her side. Her hands were close to her right thigh. As Michael got into bed, Dolores ever so softly said, "Goodnight, sweetheart."

"Good night, Dolores," Michael replied.

She already was asleep.

Michael's telephone started to ring at 6:25 AM. Apparently the first wave of early risers had recoiled at the shock of cold water.

"Yes, I know," Michael told Donna Kurland, "hot water does make a shower better."

"No, I'm sorry," Michael told Ruby Manfred, "It's unlikely that we'll get any hot water this morning."

"I'm sorry you feel that way," Michael told Jeremiah Gordon, "but I do believe these are extraordinary circumstances."

"I understand how you feel," Michael told Evelyn Ross, "but you must understand I have a different, and perhaps more accurate, view of my lineage."

At this point, Michael opened his mouth and unleashed a soundless scream. Despite his frustration, he did not want to awaken Dolores.

"I'm tired," Michael said out loud. "I've had very little sleep. I deserve sleep."

Michael adjusted the telephone answering machine so that it would pick up a call at the first ring. He adjusted the volume control downward, and returned to bed.

As he drifted off to sleep, he thought about the phone calls.

I want to help my building, thought Michael. I'm in a position where I might get killed. I can live with that. But can't I get a little sleep around here? And the insults? Why do people joke about me getting killed and want me to laugh along? It's hard to be saintly when people insist on being themselves. How does Mother Theresa do it?

Before he finally fell asleep, Michael came to a startling conclusion: I'll bet Mother Theresa is a bitch on wheels.

TWENTY-THREE

No Privacy

Sergeant Moscowitz brought his Pontiac to rest in front of the precinct. When he turned his key and the motor stopped, the stillness of the early morning hour rushed into the car.

Calvin turned his head toward the Pontiac's window and glanced at the solid gray stone precinct building.

"What happens next?" Calvin asked.

"I go home and catch a little sleep. Then I come back to my office, tanned and rested, and we talk."

"When do I sleep?" asked Calvin. "Where do I sleep?"

Moscowitz looked at Birmingham.

"You're very tired, aren't you?"

"A few Zs wouldn't hurt."

"Why don't you go home," said Moscowitz, "get your beauty rest, and then be back here no later than one o'clock this afternoon."

"You're telling me to go back to Olmsted Court?" asked Birmingham. "I don't understand. Are you going to shoot me in the back and say I escaped? You're not going to do that to me. I'm sticking right here."

"Oh, man, give me a break. You really do need some sleep. Get out of the car."

The two men opened their respective doors, and stepped into the dawn air. Calvin Birmingham started to walk into the building. Moscowitz's left hand grabbed Birmingham's right shoulder with a vise-like squeeze.

This is it, thought Birmingham. I'm going to die, just like grandma threatened so many times, at the hands of the police.

"This is not a hotel," said Moscowitz. "We have only one kind of accommodation. "If you go inside and you want to sleep, all we can offer is a jail cell cot. There's no privacy and there's lots of noise. It's the last place to be if you need some rest.

"Furthermore," Moscowitz continued, "we don't take credit cards. If you're going to sleep here, I have to arrest you. I don't want to arrest you. The paper work will prevent me from getting my sleep. And I presume you don't want to be arrested. So why don't you go home, grab your forty winks and get back here?"

"You won't shoot me in the back?"

"The paper work is even worse for that."

"Suppose I run away?"

"If that happens, I definitely get into trouble. My superiors will say unkind things to me. The media will tell the taxpayers nasty things about me. And when I find you, I'll get even.

"But that's not the point. You've already been in hiding, and you didn't like it. You would like it this time even less."

"But I can't go back to Olmsted Court. They're ready to lynch me."

"Is there anywhere else that will take you in?"

"My brother-in-law, Albert."

"Good," said Moscowitz. "Get in the car. I'll drop you off."

As the green Pontiac sped away from the station house, Calvin Birmingham smiled and closed his eyes for the first time in 48 hours.

TWENTY-FOUR

Prez Nabs Super

Dolores had done it again. Michael woke up to the smell of freshly-brewed coffee. It was a little after ten a.m. and she was sitting at the small yellow Formica table in the kitchen. Dolores already was dressed in jeans and his red-and-green plaid shirt. She had tied the shirttails at her belly. She sipped her coffee and studied the *New York Times* crossword puzzle.

Michael leaned over and kissed her on the lips.

"Good morning, honey," said Michael.

"Good morning, Michael," said Dolores.

Michael took his coffee and sat down opposite Dolores.

"I have to leave in a little while," said Dolores, "so—"

"Without making French toast?" asked the suddenly stricken Michael.

"I have to go back to my studio. Is there anything I can do for you before I go?"

"If I flashed," asked Michael, "a heartfelt leer would that be a permissible response?"

"Permissible, yes," said Dolores, "effective, no."

The doorbell rang.

The doorbell rang again.

The doorbell rang once more.

Michael opened the door and saw Louis Irving who immediately swaggered in.

"Would you like to come in?" asked Michael.

"Thank you," said Irving, ignoring the sarcasm.

"Michael," Louis Irving continued, "I'm very angry at you. Look at this."

Louis thrust a fresh copy of the *New York Post* into Michael's face. The headline screamed, "PREZ NABS SUPER."

"Give me some coffee," said Irving. "I want to hear your side of the story."

"What do you mean 'my side'?" asked Michael, even as he found himself walking into the kitchen.

Louis nodded to Dolores, and took a clean coffee mug from the dish rack. Michael poured coffee into the mug.

"I think we've met before," Louis said to Dolores.

"No we haven't," said Dolores.

"Don't you have any sugar?" Louis asked Michael.

Michael reached into a closet over the sink and extracted a few sugar packets rescued from a coffee shop.

"You do look familiar," said Louis as he sprinkled sugar into his mug. "But you're right. We never met. There was an article about you in *Popular Photography*. You're Dolores Caruso."

"You know who she is?" asked Michael.

"Of course," said Louis, "she's one of America's outstanding photographers."

"She is?"

"She is," asserted Louis. "I have two of your photographs in my collection; but I never thought I'd meet you – at least not here."

"Which pictures do you have?" asked Dolores.

"*Backstage at the High School Sing*," said Louis, "and *Ozark Broom Maker*."

"You have good taste," said Dolores. "I like both those pictures very much. What is your name again?"

"Louis. Louis Irving."

"Well, I'm pleased to meet you, Louis," said Dolores.

She turned to Michael, and said, "I've really got to go now."

She picked up her purple shoulder bag and Michael walked her to the door.

"I'm so glad you were here," said Michael.

"Me too," said Dolores.

"I'm going to be so jealous of my shirt," said Michael. "It's hugging the body of a very special woman."

They leaned toward each other and kissed. Their slowly moving hands memorized the contours of the other's body. They stepped apart and Dolores opened the door.

"Oh listen," she said. "I'm behind schedule, and I'm going to need a little bit of space—"

"A little bit of space? That's the line that women use just before they say, 'have a nice life.'"

Dolores laughed.

"Yeah," she said. "I just need a couple of days where I can concentrate on getting my show together. This project means a lot to me and I've got to do it right. Look, if there's an emergency, give me a call; but otherwise we'll talk in a few days."

"Sure," said Michael.

Dolores walked out into the hall toward the elevator.

When Michael returned to the kitchen, Louis was refilling his mug.

"Would you like another cup of coffee?" asked Michael.

"No thanks," said Louis, "I just took some."

"So you collect pictures?" said Michael.

"No," corrected Louis. "I collect fine photographic prints. All crusade and no diversion makes Louis a dull boy. I have works by Lewis Hine, Walker Evans, Eugene Smith, and Dolores Caruso."

"I never thought of you as dull," said Michael.

"I presume Dolores is not one of your patients," said Louis.

"Oh God, no," said Michael. "I think I'm her patient. She's quite something."

"She's quite a photographer," said Louis.

"I recognize a couple of the names in your collection," said Michael. "Is Dolores really as good as they are?"

"Her compositions are strong and dramatic," said Louis. "They never fail to evoke a complexity of feelings. Furthermore, her technical abilities are remarkable. She emphasizes every aspect of the photograph's meaning with her command of the tonal range – the blacks, whites and gradations of gray.

"I also like her work because it's clear that she has a strong social conscience. Besides, her prints are very affordable right now. If she becomes more established as I think she will be, my prints will be worth a bundle. If not; well, I really will not have lost much. Besides I like her pictures."

"I must admit," said Michael, "I'm looking at both Dolores and you in a new light."

"That's all well and good," said Louis Irving, pushing his coffee mug away, "I'm here to see that you look at Calvin Birmingham in a new light."

"You've got me all wrong," said Michael.

"A bunch of anonymous racists are running around saying, 'Lynch Birmingham,' and you worry about how I perceive you? Where's your sense of justice?"

"Why do you insist on slinging a word like 'racist' around?" asked Michael. "You don't really know if these people are racists. He did have that argument with Blanche."

"You've had many more arguments with Blanche," said Louis, "but I don't see your face on the cover of the *Post*. I don't see the formation of any Committee to Replace Levine."

"Believe me," said Michael, "I wish there were one. I'd become a charter member. Anyway, as I keep pointing out, Calvin is not under arrest. The police only wanted him for questioning."

"Questioning about what," demanded Louis. "Why is he the only one taken in for questioning? If they don't want to put the blame on him, just what do they want to ask him? And again, if it's no big deal, how come everybody in New York City gets told that the police were looking for him?"

"I don't know," said Michael.

"For a smart guy, you're awfully dumb," said Louis. "They're setting this guy up. And why? Because he's a black worker instead of a white boss."

"I happen to know," said Michael, "that—"

He paused. He was about to tell Louis Irving of Calvin's complicity in the Wel-Dunne scam.

"You happen to know what," demanded Louis.

"Perhaps 'know' is too definite a word," said Michael. "I happen to believe that Calvin had no role in these murders."

"You're the perfect liberal," said Louis. "You want to have your cake and eat it. All your noble statements mean nothing if you do nothing while Calvin goes to the slammer."

"What would you have me do?" asked Michael.

"You could have let Calvin get away."

"He didn't want to get away. He was tired of hiding. He only regretted that he couldn't help us with the hot water today."

"True blue," said Louis. "By the way, what is the story with the hot water?"

"What else would you have me do?"

"How should I know," said Louis, "but you are the president. There must be something you can do."

"Let me think about that," said Michael. "Meanwhile if you come up with an idea, don't hesitate to bring it to me."

"All right," said Louis. "Now, we're talking."

"I've got some stuff I've got to get to," said Michael.

"Okay," said Louis, grabbing his *Post*.

The two arose in unison and walked to the front door.

"You know," said Louis, "you, me and Dolores Caruso ought to have dinner together some time. I know this great wine bar in Clinton."

"I like that idea," said Michael. "I'll talk it over with Dolores.

"Peace, brother," said Louis.

"Right on?"

Louis slipped into the hall, and started down the stairs. Michael slowly closed the door and wondered what the rest of his day could possibly be like.

TWENTY-FIVE

Rinky Dinky Scam

Excerpts: Interrogation Of Calvin Birmingham By Sergeant Moscowitz. Homicide. Decedent(s) Herman Matterweil, Blanche Copra.

Q: State your full name and address.

A: Calvin Wilson Birmingham. 187 Eastern Parkway.

Q: Calvin, I have a good reason for wanting to question you. I happen to believe that nobody knows Olmsted Court's inner workings and behind the scenes like you know it. You know what the people there are really like. You know their secrets, their frailties and sometimes even their problems. Am I wrong?

A: No, sir.

Q: Good. But please none of this "sir" stuff. I need your help.

A: I don't know who did it.

Q: If I thought this was my lucky day, I'd buy a lottery ticket. I know you don't know who did it. Just tell me what you know about the building and the people in it, and I may hear some little nugget that helps me break the case.

A: We call the building "The Court." You know like this is the court; and the tenants, I mean the shareholders, are judge, jury and executioner.

Q: They give you a hard time?

A: They don't want to know about nothing, except their own comfort. If something goes wrong, they blame me. They don't care about the fact that I'm holding the building together with chewing gum and rubber bands, and that I've got a staff that goofs off all the time. I never have enough supplies. They don't care. It's always, "Calvin do this; Calvin do that. Calvin why didn't you do this? Calvin, why did you do that?" They're always putting money away and hiding things they don't want me to see. They do it in a sneaky way like I can't figure out what they're up to. That's their right if they want to protect their valuables. But don't treat me like I'm stupid. Some of them live like pigs; but when I make a repair, God forbid I get a speck of dust on the floor.

Q: Tell me about Herman Matterweil.

A: He was a nice enough old man. He treated me okay. When the building went co-op, I was afraid. You know, it was like the inmates took over the asylum. These people all love to power-trip. The thought of how they would act when they really had power gave me some sleepless nights. But Mr. Matterweil, he was good about it. He said that as president, he was the boss and I only had to listen to him.

Q: He was a strong-minded man?

A: He always knew what he wanted.

Q: Did that make people mad at him?

A: Oh sure, but not mad enough to kill him.

Q: Somebody didn't like Matterweil's way to play.

A: He could lean on people until they were, excuse me, red in the face and they would get real nasty back to him. But if he even whispered about resigning, they'd get down on their knees and beg him to stay on. He thought it was funny. He always laughed about it to me.

Q: Herman Matterweil made disparaging remarks about the shareholders to you?

A: Yes. I guess he had nobody else to confide in. That's kind of sad.

Q: What else did he tell you?

A: Mostly, he liked to talk about how smart he was, or how stupid everybody else was.

Q: For example?

[pause]

A: I can't think of anything else like that.

Q: Take a minute. See what comes into your mind.

[pause]

A: Sorry. It just comes up blank.

Q: You and I have to help each other, Calvin. There's a murderer running around, and I have to catch him. When I do, I'll be removing a big cloud of suspicion that's following you around.

A: I did not kill either one of them.

Q: Thank you. That's my point, exactly. You were going to tell me how Herman Matterweil boasted about being smarter than everyone else. Let me give you a hand. It had to do with the co-op, didn't it?

A: Everything has to do with the co-op with these people.

Q: But you and I know a little secret. Herman convinced everybody he was the great emancipator; but he didn't care diddly about the co-op.

A: But everyone knows he made it happen.

Q: True enough; but hardly anyone knows why. Hardly anyone knows that he set up Wel-Dunne Contractors.

A: What?

Q: Herman's little moneymaker. The contracting scam.

A: I don't —

Q: You know what I'm talking about. You were part of it.

A: Wait a minute. I knew you were going to shoot me in the back. I can't talk to you without a lawyer. Even I know that.

Q: If you get a lawyer, I'll have to arrest you, and —

A: Don't give me that bullshit about paperwork.

Q: I don't want to arrest you. I'm a homicide cop. Somebody has killed two people in the building that you run. I want to catch that killer. I don't care about some rinky dinky scam.

A: I've got to protect myself.

Q: Damned right!

A: Well.

Q: You know what goes on in the courtrooms. Your lawyer gets up and says, "Your honor, that mean mother Sergeant Moscowitz secured this confession without allowing my client to have legal counsel present. Your honor, this is a bad confession." And the judge would bang the gavel and say, "You're right, counsel, this confession sucks." You know that's the way it is.

A: Maybe. But you're a cop, and you're going to try to nail me for that crime.

Q: I'll let God have this collar if he wants it. After all, it was Matterweil's scheme. And he's figured out a way to escape me.

A: I didn't even want to do it. The night the building went co-op, he invited me to his apartment. All the cheering and handshaking in the lobby was over. Everybody else had long since gone to their apartments. He said we were going to be working together very closely and that we should share a cup of wine. That's when he told me I didn't have to listen to anyone else. It made me feel so good to hear this.

You know, before OCA dumped this co-op plan on us. Herman Matterweil acted like he didn't care if I lived or died. Then, during all those months when we were going co-op, he warmed up. He'd pat me on the back or wink at me. Sometimes he would explain things. So, when we were sitting in his apartment and sipping that wine, I felt good. Then, he started saying these things so softly, and I felt doomed.

Q: What things?

A: He said there was a lot of money to be made in this building, and he wanted me to have a share of it; but that he needed my help. He said if I would just do my job as super and hire his contracting company, everything would be just fine. He said I should lie a lot about what was needed, make it seem more drastic. He said I should look the other way when the repairs were being done. He said it wouldn't be a good idea for me to notice what materials actually were used or how long any job really took.

Q: What did you do?

A: At first, I laughed because I thought he was testing me. But he had this strange expression on his face, and I knew he really meant it. Then I tried to sound real casual. I asked, "Wouldn't it be enough to just use your contracting company, and make that money from a sweetheart deal?" He said no. He told me there was too much money to be made. He said the people in this building were stupid and lazy, and would never question the bills. He was right about that, by the way. He said he had his eye on me for a long time and he really respected me, and he wanted to see me have a chance to get something of my own, and this was the way to do it.

Q: And so that persuaded you to go along with him?

A: No! I still was afraid that if anything went wrong, I was the one who would end up on the cross. I don't have to explain why. Do I?

Q: No.

A: He said, "Calvin, you've been with the building a long time. This is a chance for you to do something for yourself. Please take it. Otherwise I have to replace you. I need somebody who will work with me." He was going to fire me. I started out in this building as a porter, and I worked my way up. And he was going to fire me just like that. I had no choice.

You know, I thought that one day, I would just get out of here, get a good building, and be a good super again. But I never did. I got too used to the whole idea.

Q: And you got too used to the money.

A: I don't think so. He didn't throw that much bread my way. I just got too used to being here, and afraid that I wasn't right for any other building

Q: Did any of the repairmen have a falling out with Matterweil?

A: No, that was the strange thing. He was a careful dude. The people who live in this building thought he was a bulldozer. And he was. He would just charge through, and flatten anybody who got in his way. But that's because he knew he could get away with it. When he needed somebody, he was very careful to stay on their right side. He always said, "Why tell people to watch out for you? If they can't figure it out, let them find out the hard way."

Q: Can you give me a list of the repairmen Wel-Dunne used?

A: Yes. It's back in my apartment.

Q: You're saying he was rougher with the shareholders than the repairmen?

A: That's right.

Q: Were there any shareholders who found out the hard way they had to watch out for him?

A: Yes.

Q: Who?

A: Mr. Krane.

Q: What about him?

A: He lives in the C-line and always complains about his back bathroom. He tells jokes all the time.

Q: So?

A: Mr. Matterweil called him a real hostile son of a bitch. That's what he called him. They had some kind of a business problem with each other years ago.

Q: A business problem?

A: They both worked at the same company. Krane used to own it, and then somehow Matterweil owned it and Krane was out on the street.

Q: How did you learn about this?

A: Mr. Matterweil bragged about it to me. He said Mr. Krane was so stupid and incompetent that he deserved to lose his company. The whole thing happened way before Krane ever moved into Olmsted Court. If you saw the two of them in the lobby you'd never suspect.

Q: So it was just a coincidence that the two ended up in the same building?

A: No. Mr. Matterweil figured that Krane hunted him down just to be in his face and to ruin his breakfast every day. He said that if Krane was a real man he never would have moved into this building.

Q: Did you ever see them argue?

A: No.

Q: Did you ever hear Krane threaten Matterweil?

A: Never.

Q: Did you ever see them together?

A: Well, sure, sometimes.

Q: What did they say? What did they do?

A: Nothing out of the ordinary. It was all surface stuff. You'd never even know they were enemies.

Q: What other shareholders did Matterweil have problems with,

A: Krane is an exception if you hear what I'm saying. He and Matterweil had their warfare outside of the building. They even kept it to themselves. The stuff that usually went on was just a lot of steam being blown off.

Q: What about the unusual?

A: Nothing really. Fights over barking dogs and parking spaces and misbehaving children. Fights over building rules.

Q: Tell me about Blanche Copra.

A: Talk about building rules, that woman wanted rules for everything — nasty rules.

Q: Did she have any enemies in the building?

A: No, not really. Most of the people here didn't pay attention to her. She'd always be scribbling on her note pad and sending out her newsletter and people would be ignoring her, laughing at her.

Q: What do you know about her personal life?

A: I didn't know she had one.

Q: Did she have any romantic relationships with other shareholders.

A: You mean sex? She didn't do the nasty with anybody. She was the nasty.

Q: What about gentleman callers?

A: Fat chance.

Q: Nobody sneaking in and out of her apartment at all hours?

A: Not that I ever noticed, and I notice a lot. She was not one of the more interesting ladies of the building. Her thing was to gripe and make trouble, and nobody took her seriously. There are really some great women in the building, and I'm not just talking about the young ones. Like Millicent Martin, I mean Dr. Martin. She's really put together and she knows it. She doesn't throw it around either. She's got this "hands off" sign that makes you want to go through red lights. She's one of that new breed of black professional women who are just straight ahead. Her only problem is that if you whisper "colored" in her ear, she'll say "where?"

Yeah, lots of great women. Roberta Haven, man. She must be pushing 60; but she really takes care of her body. It must be all that work she does in the garden. There's music in the way she moves. She's a real lady, though. But Blanche Copra? No way.

Q: Let's look at it from another angle. Maybe nobody was interested in Blanche Copra, but did she have a thing for anybody?

A: Mr. Matterweil said that she was crazy about him. But he was forever bragging about anything and everything.

Q: So you think he was just trying to make himself look good?

A: No disrespect to the dead — either one of them — but I don't see how that could make him look good in my eyes, even if it were true. Especially if it were true. She hung around him a lot. But I never saw any adoration in her eyes. She did get a bit of a glow when he said she could put one of her rules into effect.

Q: Did he have a girlfriend?

A: Not lately. There was this woman he was seeing for awhile. Every Friday afternoon, he would drive her over in his Cadillac, walk to the front door and then they'd go up-stairs. Then, every Sunday afternoon, he would have a cab take her home. They stopped going out about six months ago.

Q: Do you know why?

A: I heard her yelling something about playing second fiddle to Olmsted Court.

Q: Did she know Blanche Copra?

A: I saw the three of them together sometimes in the elevator and in the lobby. But I don't think there was any-thing of a social nature going on.

Q: When you saw them together, how did they get along?

A: This woman couldn't stand Blanche Copra. So, it was nothing out of the ordinary.

Q: What is her name?

A: Mr. Matterweil never introduced us. I guess he fig-ured I'm too socially disadvantaged to know any etiquette. But I think her name was Mrs. Fairfield or something like that.

Q: Can you tell me anything else about her?

A: Not really. I was supposed to mind my own business and keep out of her way.

Q: What about outsiders who regularly came to the building, like the mailman?

A: Oh, you mean the help?

Q: Yeah. Any beefs? Any problems, grudges?

Q: No big deal. The mailman, UPS, delivery boys, Chinese restaurants. All of them. They came in and went out. I run a tight building and there's no trouble.

A: Visitors, friends, family of shareholders, people like that?

Q: No big deal. You've got to understand that people who came here weren't involved in our bullshit. They didn't get hung up in the nonsense. They just came and went.

Q: People who came to the building on business?

A: There are none.

Q: Doesn't Michael Levine see patients?

A: I didn't think of that as business. Again, no big deal. They don't hassle us. We don't hassle them. There is this one woman. She scorches everything in front of her. And I think there's kind of a game going on between her and Archie.

Q: What's her name?

A: I don't know. Mary. Margaret. Something like that. She's one of the Monday regulars.

Q: Okay Calvin. Is there anything else you think I should know?

A: Not that I can think of. .

Q: Fine. Calvin, thank you for your cooperation. If I need you for more information, I will call on you.

A: I'll help any way I can.

TWENTY-SIX

Lady or the Tiger

At eight o'clock the next morning, Moscowitz walked briskly through the stationhouse. His tunnel vision eyes and compressed lips were a warning flare. A new file clerk, holding a cardboard blue and white coffee cup imprinted with a drawing of the Parthenon, made the mistake of greeting him.

"Good morning," she chirped.

"Die," he said softly.

The young woman flinched, spilling a few drops of coffee onto her blouse, and stepped back. She looked around for moral support. The others quickly looked away.

After Moscowitz passed, they whispered to her that it was all right; this was just his way; he meant her no harm; he merely was disturbed by some event or other.

When Moscowitz arrived at his desk, he stared at it coldly for a moment, and contemplated the hills and valleys of paper that covered its surface. His arms shot out in a butterfly stroke and his hands cast official forms, memos, pamphlets to the right and left.

He eyed the new flat plain in the middle of his desk. He found a rolled-up *New York Post* in his right hand jacket pocket and tossed the newspaper onto his desk.

"Tatum," he yelled.

There was no response. Nobody even dared to volunteer that Tatum had gone to question Krane.

"Tatum!"

No answer.

Moscowitz picked up the newspaper and waved it.

"Does anybody know what two-faced, back-stabbing, scum-sucking weasel spoke to the gentlemen of the press?"

The dead silence continued, until Delaney from vice contributed to the conversation.

"Did anyone," began Delaney, "ever tell you that you're beautiful when you're angry?"

Moscowitz spun on his heel and glared at Delaney.

The red-faced cop swallowed his smile and glared back.

The room got quieter. Moscowitz's lip twitched. His eyes closed. He began to laugh. Soon everyone in the room was laughing.

"Sorry, folks," said Moscowitz, "the press is all over us. I can't even fart without the *Post* telling all of New York that I went to the john. How am I supposed to conduct an investigation?"

Quick choruses of "yeah, right" and "those bastards" faded sweetly into the hum of normal conversation. Moscowitz eased his frame into his chair and examined the newspaper one more time.

The front page headline announced:

MYSTERY WOMAN SOUGHT
see page 5

Moscowitz again turned to page 5, although by this point he could recite the article by heart.

Suspects Mount in Horror House Slayings

Is jealousy the motive in the two grisly slayings at luxury coop Olmsted Court in the Park Slope section of Brooklyn? Or did one disgruntled businessman settle an old score? Police investigations of the violent murders of Herman Matterweil and Blanche Copra at the Eastern Parkway apartment building have turned up not one – but two – suspects, each with a different possible motive. Police have discovered that Herman Matterweil had a mistress. According to one new police theory, she may be a green-eyed monster who stalked the building. Her identity is still unknown; but the mystery woman and Matterweil met every weekend until they had a falling out. She resented the way building matters interfered with their weekend trysts.

"It was more than plumbing," said one source close to the investigation. "She decided that Matterweil and Blanche Copra were fooling around, and she didn't like it one bit."

Investigators do not yet know the mystery woman's name or whereabouts; but they are doubling their efforts to find her.

The other suspect, a business executive, actually lives in Olmsted Court. Although police would not release his name, reliable sources indicate he is a vice-president of sales for a leading housewares manufacturer. Twelve years earlier, the businessman and Matterweil were involved in a business deal that went sour. The businessman lost his job and investment and blamed Matterweil for these losses.

In another development, the building's superintendent, Calvin Birmingham, who gave himself up for questioning, was released after questioning by the police.

"Why won't these jerkoffs just let me do my job?" wondered Moscowitz. "Tatum!"

The oft-requested Officer Tatum had just entered Olmsted Court, and been greeted by Archie.

"What do you think," asked Archie, "was it the dame or the salesman? My money's always on the dame."

It was still in the midst of the morning shopping hour, and the elevator door opened. A swarm of hunters and gatherers stepped into the lobby, en route to the front door. Each studied a sheet of Xerox paper. As the residents approached the doorman's station, Archie and Tatum could make out the characteristic appearance of the New York Post headline and article.

"Isn't that nice," said Archie, "someone made copies of the Post article, and distributed it. I tell you these people are always helping one another."

Let's hope, thought Tatum, that nobody helps Moscowitz. He hates seeing this stuff.

"So who is it," asked Archie, "the lady or the tiger?"

"The lady or the tiger?"

"Who's our killer? Who's running amok?"

"How should I know?" replied Tatum. "Why don't you ask somebody in a better position to know, like a newspaper reporter? I'm just here to do a job. What apartment is Frederick Krane in?"

"So you don't think Matterweil's sweetie did it?"

"The apartment number, please."

The intercom at Archie's station buzzed loudly.

"Keep your shirt on," said Archie. Looking at Tatum, he added, "7A."

"Thanks," said Tatum, who walked toward the elevator.

"Don't mention it," said Archie, as he deigned to pick up the intercom. "Hello."

Archie listened to the obviously excited shareholder at the other end.

"Right away, sir," said Archie who then hung up.

"Oh, officer," yelled Archie.

"What," said Tatum.

"I'm told that Mr. Krane is on the roof."

"What?"

The elevator door opened; more people came out.

"Mr. Kempton, the guy who owns the penthouse just called down," said Archie. "Krane is on the roof, and he's dancing, and he's buck naked."

"Oh Christ," said Tatum, entering the elevator. "Call 911. How do I get to the roof?"

"Go to the top floor and through the penthouse."

Archie turned to the telephone as the elevator door closed.

"Buck naked and dancing," said Archie, "I don't know which is a more chilling image."

Tatum's knock on the penthouse door was greeted by a male voice from inside.

"Yes?"

"Police."

"I just called downstairs. Response time should be six minutes at the least. This is too fast. You won't catch me opening the door."

"I was in the building," said Tatum.

"Show me your badge."

Tatum fumbled for his wallet, opened it and showed his NYPD badge. Kempton hesitated.

"Let's go, let's go, let's go," barked Tatum.

Bolts were snapped apart and the door quickly opened,

"Which way," said Tatum.

The man's finger pointed through the living room to an open door. Tatum rushed through the living room, and stepped gingerly through the door that led to the roof. Strange sounds came from the right. Tatum heard irregular footstomping, and loud mumbling, intermingled with the panting that comes from heavy exertion. Krane the salesman was just around the penthouse's corner. Tatum walked softly, not wishing to alarm the man.

Krane was engrossed in his grotesque dance, and he was emphatically, blatantly naked. That was not the worst of it. What Tatum interpreted as mumbling really was singing.

"Mr. Krane," said Tatum.

"In a Gadda Davida, baby," replied Krane.

Wilhelmina Fairfield sat at the dining room table of her Park Avenue apartment. She sipped coffee from a pale green bone china teacup, and studied the *New York Post* one more time. She reached for the phone and called her lawyer.

"Marilyn," she said, "do you remember that beast in Brooklyn I was seeing?"

"Yes."

"First he seduced me, then he debased me. That wasn't too bad. But then he bored me. But now, this is too much."

"What happened?"

"The beast screwed me."

Wilhelmina Fairfield read the *New York Post* article to her lawyer.

"Stay there," said the lawyer, "and don't talk to anybody without me."

"Of course; but I had so wanted to go shopping today."

TWENTY-SEVEN

Our Pink Flamingo

Tatum stepped out of the elevator first. Krane the salesman, modestly draped in a blue and beige floral print sheet, followed. Two burly uniformed police officers, one clutching each of Krane's arms, seriously impaired his choreographic aspirations. Dennis Kempton trailed. Krane's hands, hidden by the sheet, were cuffed behind his back. Krane managed to sneak in a few jig steps as he was hustled through the lobby. Archie swung the front door open with a flourish as the parade approached him. When Krane was pulled across the doorway, he glanced over his shoulder, laughed, and shouted, "Top of the world, Ma. Top of the world."

Archie watched as the two cops and Tatum maneuvered Krane into the back seat of the blue-and-white patrol car. The car sped away, and Kempton walked slowly into Olmsted Court.

"I always knew that guy was crazy," said Archie, "but I never realized until now that he's also a nut."

"I'm the crazy one," said Kempton. "I let them have that sheet, and I didn't get a receipt for it."

Within ten minutes, the echoes of Krane's songs and shouts had vanished. A double-parked blue and white patrol car, an homage to the crime scene, could have been waiting innocently for a speeder.

Teenage boys and girls, leaning against a sky blue Toyota station wagon, listened thoughtfully to the flow of rap music coming from the boom box. The boys, one at a time, emerged from the group to do a tricky dance step. Each, at the conclusion of his solo, flashed a macho smile at the girls. It was the role of the girls to make disparaging observations, giggle, and turn away.

The sense of normalcy was emphasized by Roberta Haven. She was at her familiar station, working on the patch of green in front of the building – the Olmsted Court "garden." This morning, she was lending an air of industry by trimming the hedges with an electric saw.

Ruby Manfred, newspaper clutched under his arm, was returning to the building from his morning stroll. He paused to watch Roberta.

"Our pink flamingo strikes again," he said warmly.

The statement made Roberta Haven smile ever so slightly. It reminded her that Mr. Krane coined the term "our pink flamingo" in a burst of inspiration on a morning very much like this one.

"Hey," Krane had said to whomever was standing near him, "other buildings get pink flamingos to decorate their lawns. We get Roberta Haven. I think we lucked out."

Henceforth, Krane and occasionally others referred to Roberta as "our pink flamingo." She immediately understood it as a term of affection. Once, she even had been captivated by a witty thought.

"Why, Mr. Krane," she said, "I do believe this is a case of the Krane calling the flamingo pink."

He stared blankly.

"Crane...flamingo," she explained. "They're both wading birds."

"Right," he said.

Poor Mr. Krane, thought Roberta Haven. And the poor man is totally naked under that sheet. She blushed and returned to her work as Ruby Manfred entered Olmsted Court.

While Manfred strolled through the building's lobby, Walter, who was at his office, telephoned Michael with a Krane report. Michael had been showering at the time of the Krane episode and knew nothing of the matter.

"No kidding," said Michael. "He actually said 'top of the world, Ma?'"

"You have training in the field," said Walter. "What happened?"

"I'd say that he went bananas," said Michael.

"I know that. But why? Was it the article in the *Post*?"

"Walter how could I give an opinion? I haven't really studied this case."

"I didn't mean to insult you. I was just curious."

"Okay, let me try to think about it out loud," said Michael. "You know how Krane was forever telling his jokes. And he was so intense about it."

"Yes," said Walter. "Grim city. It gave me the willies."

"I don't know why we're using the past tense," said Michael. "Anyway, there's that chestnut about humor being a form of hostility. If so, he was – is – one hostile sonofabitch. If we can believe that newspaper article, Herman did him wrong, and that's a good explanation for his hostility."

"That accounts for his jokes," said Walter, "but why was he up on the roof doing the dance of the no veils?"

"This is a wild guess," answered Michael, "and I won't even bill you for it; but let's presume he's been carrying this anger about Herman all these years. All of a sudden Herman is killed violently. Perhaps, he feels responsible. Perhaps, he feels his rage killed Herman."

"Perhaps," said Walter, "his rage really did kill Herman."

"I don't know about that," said Michael, "but we're trying to find out what got him to the roof. We know he's got all this rage. What happens to this hostility when Herman is removed from the scene?"

"Well, he's got nothing to be angry about," said Walter, "so I guess he can take it easy now."

"Could be," said Michael, "except that often when people are angry toward others, it's a sign that they feel anger toward themselves. They don't acknowledge it. Bye-bye Herman, and now Krane has to acknowledge it. He's in denial, and then, boom out comes the newspaper that says, 'this guy may be guilty.' The article affirms the guilt he already feels. He wants to cast off this feeling that is so tied to his persona. So, he decides he can shed his identity by shedding his clothes."

"That's bizarre," said Walter.

"It's amazing what the human psyche will do."

"I meant that your explanation is bizarre."

Michael was stung.

"You're free," he said, "to get a second opinion."

A wailing fire engine siren gently slipped into Michael's consciousness.

"You know I didn't mean anything personal, Michael. Anyway, the only reason I called was because we may have to do something about this Krane business."

Michael heard another sound; but he couldn't quite identify it.

"What are we supposed to do?" asked Michael.

"There are two aspects. First, we should tell share-holders that the killer has been apprehended, and they can come out now. At least that's my opinion."

What was that sound?

"How can we say that? We don't know if Krane is the killer."

It wasn't exactly a sound.

"The other part is that Krane may be out of commission for awhile and unable to pay his maintenance. If he falls behind, when should we foreclose?"

Actually, it was a sound and then a non-sound — a sound and the stopping of a sound. It was the sound of heavy trucks stopping — heavy trucks, such as tractor-trailers or fire engines.

"Gotta go, Walter. Good-bye."

By the time Michael arrived downstairs, the lobby was covered with raincoat-wearing firefighters, immersed in their tasks. Several, holding a giant fire hose, were running toward the fire stairs. A stocky firefighter concentrated on the crackling knowledge that emerged from his walkie-talkie.

"Nothing in the boiler room," he heard.

Another firefighter, obviously an officer, was talking with Archie. The doorman continually shrugged and shook his head. The officer stepped away, scanned the lobby, summoned two other firefighters to his side, and waved his arm. All the firefighters stopped, and seemed to go into reverse. Carrying their equipment, they drifted outside.

"What happened?" Michael asked one of the exiting firefighters.

"False alarm," he was told.

It's not a crisis, thought Michael. What a relief. It's an occasion.

Sergeant Moscowitz sat on a scratched maple chair next to Dr. Maria Escobar's gray metal desk on the third floor of Kings County Hospital's G Building. Moscowitz was impressed, and perhaps intimidated by the neatness of her desktop. He watched her scribble entries in the spaces of a multi-page printed form. She wore an open long white uniform over a high-collared rust dress. When she completed her notations, she capped her fountain pen, and looked at Moscowitz.

"What else do you need, Sergeant Moscowitz?" she asked.

"When can I question Krane?"

"Oh," she said, "I do believe we'll be holding his calls for awhile."

"There's a homicide case going on here."

"Tell me about it. Right now, the man's got oatmeal for brains. If something happens I'll let you know."

"I need something now."

"I'm sure you can find some other killing to look into." Moscowitz stood.

"When something happens," he said, "give me a call."

On the building's main floor, Moscowitz found a pay-phone that worked.

"Tatum, tell them to hurry up and find Matterweil's love slave" he said, "and you meet me at the coffee shop."

TWENTY-EIGHT

What a Bummer

At 3:30 p.m. fire engines returned to Olmsted Court for the fourth time that day.

"Some kid's been turning in false alarms," said Archie to everyone. "It's got to be a kid. Nobody else does that kind of thing."

A restless Michael Levine sat on his comfortable living room wingback chair but felt no peace.

Grandma would say I have no *zeitflesh*, he thought. It's all this building stuff. All these false alarms. Somebody is waging psychological warfare against us. Isn't murder bad enough? Ugh. Murder, What a bummer! I can't just sit here. I'll check out the building and see if anything weird is going on. Anything weird besides me.

At his front door, he grabbed the same baseball bat he had held tightly the night he and Dolores found Calvin Birmingham eating fried chicken.

Michael started at the roof and methodically proceeded down. He would search for anomalies, listen for strange sounds, be alert to danger. And most of all, he would pretend that he always strolled through the building with a baseball bat in his hands.

In the empty laundry room washing machine number three held a load of towels that needed transfer to a dryer. In the boiler room, Michael paused to admire the great natural gas-fed furnace blasting forth its heat. As he advanced toward the compactor room, he heard muffled but excited voices.

I suppose, he thought, the porters have discovered another body, but I kind of hope not.

Entering the compactor room, Michael saw two men engrossed in their tasks. The shorter of the two neatly scattered discarded newspapers about the room. The other generously poured kerosene across the paper.

"Hey," Michael shouted, "What are you doing?"

"Go away," said the taller, "we're working."

The shorter man drew a knife. Michael gasped.

I'm going to be hurt, he thought. Have to protect myself.

Michael blindly swung the bat, and actually connected with the shorter man's wrist. The knife flew harmlessly to the floor. The taller man shook the kerosene can, and a few remaining drops of fluid dropped out. He turned toward Michael. The two men and Michael circled each other warily in the cramped space.

This is easy, thought Michael.

He waved the bat in front of him to keep the interlopers at a distance.

"Ahh hell," said the shorter man. "I've got an appointment."

Dropping his head, as if he were dodging a low ceiling, he threw his arm out and grabbed the bat. Then he kicked

Michael in the crotch. The taller man quickly punched Michael in the ribs and then brought the kerosene can down on Michael's head. Hard! Michael wilted and fell.

The taller man picked up the baseball bat and said, "Let's get out of here."

"What about the fire?"

"I'll do arson, not murder."

"I agree in principle," said the shorter man, "but we get paid to do a job, we should do it. I guess I got an old-fashioned work ethic."

"Don't worry. We'll be back. Let's go."

As they briskly walked out, the taller man said, "It's not a total loss. My kid's been busting my chops for a baseball bat. Now he's got one."

Then they were gone.

Michael lay there for a few minutes. He knew he had to get back up; but the pain, streaming up from different body parts, hypnotized him. Finally, the kerosene's pungent scent annoyed him more than the pain subdued him. Michael struggled to his feet. He staggered into the elevator, pressed "1", and slumped in a corner of the elevator cab.

They took my baseball bat, he thought. My bat. Mommy gave me that bat. I hit a home run with that bat.

Michael smiled when he saw Archie's familiar form.

"Archie," Michael said when he reached the doorman's station.

Archie's nostrils dilated.

"Have you been painting, Mr. Levine?" asked Archie.

""Did you see two men with a baseball bat leave here?"

"Two men with a baseball bat?"

"Yes," said Michael.

"No," said Archie. "Were those the same two guys who were looking for you?"

"What?"

"Yeah, two guys were looking for you," continued Archie. "They said they had to pick something up. You didn't answer the intercom, so I sent them up."

"When there's no answer, you're not supposed to send them up. That's why we have an intercom."

"I was just trying to help."

"Thanks!" said Michael. "They beat me up."

"That's too bad," said Archie.

"I'll be upstairs if I'm needed," said Michael.

"Good," replied Archie. "I'll pass the word on."

Once again, Michael felt protected by his apartment. He also felt an incredible headache. In his bathroom, he examined the aspirin bottle and wondered: When did I buy these? Are they still good?

Michael swallowed two aspirins and went to the kitchen to phone Moscowitz. Miraculously, it seemed, the sergeant was in. Michael spilled out all the information about the false alarm and the two men who were about to start a fire.

"Oh, that's who they are," said Moscowitz, "One of our uniforms collared one of them. He saw the perp running out of your building's side entrance and holding onto a real sad-looking baseball bat. That was suspicious enough to him. So, you saw them trying to set a fire? That's great. Come down and identify the man."

"Sure," said Michael.

He hung up, walked slowly into the living room and sat in his chair.

Just a week ago, he thought, the closest I got to life was listening to other people's stories. But now I've been beaten up and almost barbecued. No wonder I'm ready for romance.

TWENTY-NINE

Too Much Crime

Michael pretended to look purposeful as he entered the precinct house.

I'm out of place here, he thought. Just like I am in hardware stores. Everybody else is buying heavy-duty tools or strange pieces of metal that they know how to use, and I'm studying a Melita coffeemaker or a small pot to boil my eggs in. And they all know I don't belong there. Okay, I acknowledge my feelings; but I'm here in the public interest. I'm here to ID a perp, or whatever they call it. I was going to use my skills to find the murderer. I was going to do it for Herman, for the building, for me, for Andre, for civilization. And now I'm squeamish about just telling what I witnessed.

Look at all these cops, he thought. I must have done something wrong. Otherwise why would I be here? They have ways of seeing your guilt. What was it Moscowitz said? "Confess. You'll feel better."

A police officer behind a long wooden counter sorted a large pile of forms. Another officer, wearing a pleasant smile, was deep in conversation with a woman standing to Michael's left. She clearly was not a cop.

"What kind of person," she asked, "would sneak into my store when it's closed, and trash it?"

"Not a taxpayer," he genially replied.

The officer sorting forms looked up and made eye contact with Michael.

"Excuse me," said Michael, "how can I locate the detectives?"

The policeman yawned.

"If you want to find out about a stolen car," he said, "call this phone number—" he slipped a small Xeroxed phone form toward Michael, "—and they'll help you."

"I'm not here for a stolen car," said Michael. "I'm here for a homicide, the one the papers call the co-op murders"

"Hmm," said the police officer. "That's heavy stuff. The guys handling that are on the second floor. Take the elevator over there."

"Are there stairs I can use?"

"Stairs are off-limits to citizens. Too much crime."

When the elevator doors closed behind him, Michael found himself in a large open area. The hunt and peck typewriter staccato and constant ringing of telephones made him feel he was on the set of a very bad television show. Moscowitz, seated at a desk, was studying the contents of a file folder. The sergeant concentrated so intently that an invisible shield seemed to surround him and his desk. All chatter bounced helplessly off the shield and broke into particles. Moscowitz smiled when he noticed Michael.

Moscowitz led Michael through a series of hallways and closed doors labeled "Authorized Personnel Only." They reached their apparent destination. It resembled a conference room, and its main feature was a drawn window shade on a wall where there could not be a window. Moscowitz slowly raised the shade, and to Michael's amazement, there was a window. It showed the vast panorama of an adjacent room. Michael saw a familiar face. It was the taller arsonist.

"Oh wait a minute," said Michael.

"Not to worry," said Moscowitz.

The arsonist fussed and fretted with a pack of Marlboro cigarettes, and never seemed to notice Michael.

"One-way glass?" asked Michael.

Moscowitz nodded.

"I take it from your reaction," said Moscowitz, "that you recognize this man?"

"Yes," said Michael "That's the bastard who stole my baseball bat."

"We're investigating a homicide, not the theft of your baseball bat."

"My mother gave it to me."

"I understand," said Moscowitz. "What action specifically did you see this man performing in your compactor room?"

"He had this can of gasoline or some awful smelling stuff and was pouring it. The other guy was spreading newspapers out on the floor and they were just saturating the newspapers with this stuff."

"Good," said Moscowitz.

"Is he the murderer?" asked Michael.

"I don't think so," said Moscowitz. "but he's got to be a real big finger pointing straight at a bad guy. His name is

Ernie Carson. He's been linked with a whole slew of apartment house arsons; although he hasn't been indicted for any. Carson is a member of the Building Employees Union."

As the two ambled through the doorways back to Moscowitz's desk, a thought struck Michael.

"Wouldn't," Michael began, "Calvin Birmingham be a member of the same union?"

"I suppose."

"So, they might know each other?"

"It's possible," said Moscowitz.

"Then, doesn't that mean that Calvin is a suspect again?"

"I don't think it's appropriate for me to answer that question."

"Oh, no," said Michael.

"There's also the matter of 'Operation Whacko'"

"What?"

"Herman Matterweil put all the correspondence that annoyed him into a folder labeled 'The Whacko File.' Some of your letters are in it. We have to check out people who earned a spot in the Whacko file."

The two walked silently until they reached Moscowitz's desk. The piles of paper that had been strewn about during his rage reoccupied the terrain. Moscowitz handed the "Please leave lovers alone" letter to Michael.

"What does this mean?" the cop asked.

"I don't know," said Michael, studying the letter. "It's poignant and yet Herman just scribbled all over it. The small, precise script suggests somebody in a constant state of self-control."

He looked at the letter again.

"Is this a clue?"

"Probably not," said Moscowitz. "But it's the only letter in the file about leaving lovers alone. And it's not signed. And then there's that note on it. Matterweil may have figured out the letter-writer's identity and made an appointment with him."

"What," Moscowitz continued, "is your diagnosis of the whacko file, doc?"

Michael stared at the file one more time, and shook his head.

"Therapy might have helped," said Michael "If your killer is hiding in that pile, therapy might even have saved Herman's life."

Michael stood, preparing to leave.

"One more thing," said Moscowitz. "Details of this investigation keep ending up in the newspaper, and it's really giving me a pain."

"I haven't said anything."

"I'm sure you haven't," said Moscowitz, "but I'd like to pursue these leads without the pressure of reading inaccuracies about them."

"I certainly wouldn't—"

"I know. You don't want the papers to report we're investigating your patients."

"You're not—"

"Not yet. Maybe we won't the way things are going. But if we do, I don't want it reported and you don't want it reported; just like I don't want anything we discussed today about Ernie Carson to get reported. As the saying goes, you I trust completely. It's the person you tell that I have a problem with. Will this be our little secret?"

Please let them find the murderer soon, thought Michael.

"Deal," said Michael.

As he walked out of the station house, Michael felt relieved.

That wasn't so bad, he thought. Maybe now I should go to a hardware store.

THIRTY

Screw Freud

I was almost barbecued, thought Michael as he walked home from the police station. Barbecued. What an image. And yet I seem to care more about the baseball bat. It must be the blow on the head. But my mommy gave me that bat. My mommy gave me that bat? How Freudian can you get?

Oh, screw Freud! Screw Freud? The master would just love that sentiment. Can't I just love the bat because it was a gift from my mother? Does it have to mean something else?

One April morning when he was 11-years-old, Michael discovered his new baseball bat on the kitchen table next to the brown paper bag that held his lunch. Michael inhaled deeply and walked softly to the table. His hand reached out gently to claim the prize. His fingers stretched toward the Willie Mays signature, and then they drew back quickly as if touching flame. Maybe this was not his. There was no gift-wrapping, no message, no note, and there had been no hint in the days before that the bat was going to appear.

It was his. It had to be his. It was next to his lunch, waiting for school to start. He took it. A mixed cocktail of joy and guilt spread through his system. What bliss it was to have this splendid bat. But suppose it didn't belong to him. It was his. It had to be his.

A few days earlier while bringing the groceries in, he talked with his mother about his love for baseball.

"I'm cut out to be a shortstop," he reported, "but I need to work on my hitting. I need to get more pop on the ball."

"I'm sure you will," she said. "You just have to work on it."

"Do you know what pop on the ball is?" Michael asked his mother.

"Not really," she replied, "but I know it's something you need, and something you'll work on. I'm sure you could do it, if you really try hard."

Was she saying he could do it or he never would do it? He wasn't sure.

"Pop means power," he said. "I can make contact and get wood on the ball. It just doesn't go far."

"Give it time. I'm sure it will."

"I need a bat," said Michael. "All the bats in school stink. Stan Rosenblatt has his own bat, and he gets lots of hits."

"Maybe you could use his bat," Michael's mother suggested.

"No, you don't understand," said Michael. "It's his bat. He works with it. He knows it. Just like Willie Mays, his bat is an extension of his hands. He practices swinging it all the time."

"I see," said his mother. "It's very interesting. Now let's finish with these groceries."

And that was that, until the bat appeared on the kitchen table. He let the bat rest on his shoulder as if he were on deck and peering at the pitcher. He spied his mother entering the room. He flinched, and she smiled.

"Did I get the right one, darling?" she asked.

"Oh yes, oh yes."

He, while holding the bat with one hand, threw his other arm around her waist.

Michael took the baseball bat with him to school that morning, and all his friends were impressed. They predicted great things for him. He let them touch the bat. After all, they were his friends. He even let them swing the bat a couple of times.

At recess time, he ran into the schoolyard, and then suddenly stopped. Suppose he fell and scratched the bat. He walked quickly. When home plate was in sight, he ran and ran holding the bat aloft.

He didn't get a hit with his new bat that day; but he did drive the ball further than he ever had before. In the weeks to come, he practiced and did get hits. He even got a home run. What a wonderful bat.

THIRTY-ONE

Jogging in the First Degree

Mascowitz stared at his desktop, and shifted his weight in his chair. He studied the letters in Herman Matterweil's whacko file. It was not a pleasant task. A grinning Tatum appeared at his side.

"I've got some good news and some bad news," said Tatum.

"The good news," said Moscowitz, "is that you're not directing traffic in Staten Island."

"Shame, shame. Not even close."

Tatum placed a sheet of paper on Matterweil's desk.

"I got this from the union," said Tatum. "It's a list of our pyro's employers. See the one I underlined?"

Moscowitz moved his finger down the list and stopped abruptly at Tatum's bold penciled line.

"Bingo," said Moscowitz softly, "Olmsted Court Associates, the building's landlord before it went co-op. This says he's still working for them."

"Here's the best part," said Tatum. "Look at Carson's other jobs."

Once again, Moscowitz dragged his finger along the list. He saw a string of different realty firms. All had the same Brooklyn Heights address, OCA's address.

"So," said Moscowitz, "some business that owns a lot of property and used to own Olmsted Court has this guy on its payroll. Why are they involved in this building now, and how is this involvement related to the murders?

"You said," he continued, "you have bad news. What is it?"

"Carson's attorney just blew in."

"Let me guess," said Moscowitz. "He's wearing an expensive suit, and he's a partner in a law firm that has a lot of juice."

"Carnac the Magnificent strikes again," said Tatum, handing Moscowitz the attorney's business card.

"That may not be bad news. Let's check him out."

Ernie Carson sat in the interrogation room with his lawyer. The lawyer, wearing a black pinstripe suit, sat calmly and practiced his smile. He kept his manicured hands on his crossed knees, as if he were taking great pains to avoid touching anything remotely sooty. Carson kept squirming in his seat as if he were once again in the principal's office.

As the two policemen entered the room, Moscowitz extended his right hand and glanced quickly at the business card in his left hand. The attorney sprang to his feet and offered his right hand.

"Hello, Mr. – uh – Rattner," said Moscowitz. "I'm Sergeant Moscowitz, and this is Officer Tatum."

"Sheldon Rattner, at your service."

"At someone's service," said Moscowitz dryly.

"Sergeant," said Rattner, "I must say that after talking with my client, I'm a bit disturbed. He was detained for running out of the side entrance of a building. I know of no statute that covers jogging in the first degree."

"He was carrying a baseball bat," said Tatum.

"Oh, well then, that explains everything. If you see a man running, and he's carrying a piece of sports equipment, obviously he must be arrested."

"You're twisting everything up," said Tatum.

"I'm just describing what happened," said Rattner. "It's the penetrating light of day that makes it sound twisted to you."

"Penetrating light of day," repeated Tatum, "you're wasting some good poetry on a lowlife client."

"Tatum," said Moscowitz reprovingly, "Mr. Rattner is here to do his job. Insulting him or his client does not make our job any easier."

"But Sergeant—"

"Please Tatum," said Moscowitz. "I'm sorry, Mr. Rattner, please continue."

"Thank you, Sergeant. As I understand it, your uniformed police officers chose, in their infinite wisdom, to detain Mr. Carson. They did so for no tangible reason. They were not responding to a crime report, nor had they come across a crime in progress. They saw Mr. Carson running, and they did not like it."

"This is bullshit," said Tatum.

"Tatum," said Moscowitz. "Shut up or get out."

Tatum glumly sat down in a chair opposite Carson.

"Mr. Rattner," said Moscowitz, "although Officer Tatum's manner is less than respectful, I believe he was going to make an excellent point. Your client was not running out of any old building. He was running out of Olmsted Court, the site of a murder investigation."

"And you're charging him with homicide?"

"Well, no," said Moscowitz.

Rattner performed an exaggerated shrug. His palms faced heaven as if to signify that only Jehovah could understand these earthly events.

"We asked him what he was doing and first he said nothing then he said he was visiting a friend but he wouldn't give us the friend's name."

"The friend is a lady," said Rattner, "who has – um – other commitments. He sees no reason to create problems for her."

"Sergeant—" protested Tatum.

"You're holding my client for no apparent reason," said Rattner. "Unless, of course, you're trying to create a smoke screen because – how shall I put it – your highly visible homicide investigation has been less than fruitful."

"Very diplomatic, Mr. Rattner," said Moscowitz. "I can see why you're so successful."

"Please release Mr. Carson," said Rattner.

"I really resent it," said Moscowitz, "when some hotshot lawyer comes into my office and throws his weight around."

"I understand," said Rattner, "and if I were in your position I would have the same resentment. Now, please release my client."

"Come on," said Moscowitz, "Carson isn't your client. Some fat cat is. Somebody who finds it inconvenient for Carson to be here."

"If that's how you'd like to view the situation," said Rattner, "fine. Obviously, Mr. Carson does not have the means to engage the kind of representation, my firm customarily provides. It is my understanding that the man is a hard worker and a loyal worker. He has the kind of work ethic that made this country great. The party who asked me to appear here applauds this kind of devotion, and hates to see injustice being done. Will you please release my client, or shall I phone the City Editor of the *New York Post.*"

"I hate it," said Moscowitz, "but you've got me over a barrel."

"I don't believe this," said Tatum.

"I know," said Moscowitz, "but it's the system."

Moscowitz turned to Rattner and said, "I'll check with my lieutenant."

"You do that, Sergeant."

Moscowitz and Tatum left the room, and quietly walked through the corridors. At last Tatum spoke.

"What about the arson? We have him on that. Why don't we hold him on that?"

"We know we've got that; but apparently, they don't. Why should we tell them?"

"But, if we've got him, we can question him, and we can get—"

"Bupkis," said Moscowitz. "We get nothing with this attorney standing around. Let's do it the easy way. Tell Taylor to follow Carson. I think he will lead us to Olmsted Court Associates incarnate. When Taylor is ready to go, release Carson."

"I like it." said Tatum.

"Also in the Copra collection, aren't there some kind of forms that all the tenants – I beg your pardon – shareholders – filled out?"

"Yes."

"Check the handwriting on those forms to see if any match this 'leave lovers alone' note."

Three hours later, Tatum had another piece of paper for Moscowitz.

"We now know Carson's favorite dry cleaner and grocery store," said Tatum. "Judging from the items he bought he seems to be watching his cholesterol. But here's the bulls-eye. He made a long stop at this private residence in Brooklyn Heights. It's a nice expensive pad and it looks out on the river. My favorite part is the address."

Moscowitz looked at the sheet of paper.

"Ahh, the OCA mother ship," Moscowitz said. "Who owns it?"

"No personal name registered," said Tatum, "Only a corporation. But Taylor questioned a D'Agostino's supermarket delivery boy. The occupant is one Herman Calloway."

"Why is that name familiar?"

"He's better known as Archie."

"Olmsted Court's doorman?"

"He keeps a low profile, alright," said Tatum, "we did some more checking and his corporations make him one of New York City's leading slumlords. He's pretty ruthless. He routinely uses lawyers and muscle to make life lousy for his tenants. He apparently had something different in mind for Olmsted Court."

"I think we should discuss real estate with Mr. Calloway."

THIRTY-TWO

A Sweet Idea

Michael woke to an amiable Spring morning that washed all of Brooklyn with a peach glow and lit every corner of his apartment. Across the street from Olmsted Court, the Botanic Gardens swayed from the impact of bright blossoms, newly burst into color and fragrance. Without shame, guile or regard for havoc, they tossed their perfume into the air. The garden planted a sweet idea in Michael's mind and he immediately phoned Dolores.

"Come to Brooklyn," he crooned. "Come to Brooklyn."

"Why?" she asked.

"Cherry Blossoms," he replied.

"Okay," she said.

Michael and Dolores were strolling in the Brooklyn Botanic Garden just before noon. Her capped Minolta camera hung about her neck. The sun's warmth brought a slight patina of sweat to Dolores and Michael's brows and calm to their faces. Some parents and their 10-year-old children pantomimed a baseball game and thus evaded the "no ballplaying allowed" rule.

As the couple walked casually through Cherry Lane, Michael kept nodding to his fellow Olmsted Courters who also were enjoying the garden. When the duet neared Daffodil Hill, Michael noticed Roberta Haven seated on a bench. She and a garden maintenance worker were talking animatedly.

"I bet they're talking about fertilizer," said Michael.

"It doesn't look like that to me," said Dolores. Her elbow softly nudged Michael in the ribs.

"You mean," began Michael. "Oh no, not her. Roberta? No. All she cares about is gardening."

"Look at their faces change expression while they talk," said Dolores. "What an interesting looking couple."

She raised the Minolta to her left eye, and released the shutter.

When Roberta heard the Minolta's loud click, she turned in panic, and then quickly composed herself.

"Why hello, Mr. Levine, I don't believe I've met your friend before."

"Roberta Haven," said Michael, "this is Dolores Caruso. Dolores, Roberta."

The Botanic Garden maintenance worker abruptly stood.

"My name is Jerry," he said, "and I have to get back."
He turned to Roberta.

"Maybe we can finish our conversation later," he said.

"Maybe," she replied.

He was gone.

"I hope I didn't break your camera," said Roberta.

"No," said Dolores. "You look just lovely."

"I wish you hadn't taken my picture."

"It'll be lovely," assured Dolores.

"I don't like my picture taken at certain times," said Roberta. "I don't like it. You know there are times I just like to be left alone.

Roberta sighed, and then continued, "Do you ever photograph flowers."

"Not generally. I'm a people person."

"I've been photographing flowers for more than 20 years," said Roberta. "They're not like people. They're more modest."

Dolores squeezed Michael's hand.

"I'm afraid we have to go back now," he told Roberta.

Michael and Dolores briskly retraced their steps, and soon had passed through the ornate metal gate that separated the Botanic Garden from the outside world.

As they crossed Eastern Parkway, they noticed three patrol cars, their revolving cherry lights flashing, idling nervously in front of Olmsted Court. Michael dashed into the building, and saw handcuffs being placed on Archie's wrists.

"What are you doing?" asked Michael. "He's been with us for years."

"Tell me about it," says Moscowitz.

THIRTY-THREE

There's No Percentage in Murder

A crowd of residents quickly bloomed. They looked at Archie with curiosity, and whispered his name. Michael heard the soft chant, "Free Archie; free Archie."

"Wait a minute, Sergeant," said Michael. "What are you doing with our doorman?"

"Oh," said Moscowitz, "we thought we'd like to give him a tour of our precinct. You know the man is very interested in real estate."

The chant got louder.

"Sergeant—" said Michael.

"You," said Moscowitz, "are asking about Herbert Calloway a/k/a Archie the doorman a/k/a owner of Olmsted Court Associates."

"OCA," said Michael, "our old landlord?"

He turned to the doorman.

"Archie," he said, "is this true?"

"Who're you going to believe," asked Archie, "me or some cop?"

People in the front of the crowd chewed on this startling piece of information. The news had not spread to the rear where the chant of "Free Archie" continued.

"But," said Michael, "you told me OCA was owned by a bunch of big shot Long Island doctors who hated Brooklyn."

"So?"

"You lied to me," said Michael.

"This guy is hopeless," said Archie to the cops. "Get me out of here."

The chant had completely evaporated, and the crowd had broken into small discussion groups clustered around the lobby.

"Your friend," Moscowitz told Michael, "who took your baseball bat works for Mr. Calloway."

"My baseball bat," said Michael, "when do I get that back?"

"We'll have to work that out," said Moscowitz. "As I was saying, your Mr. Calloway has a number of properties."

"Olmsted Court was always my favorite," said Archie. "I like the way it was built. That's why I worked here, so I can keep an eye on it."

"And start rumors," added Moscowitz, "and pretty much destabilize the place. Everybody talks to Archie, and Archie spreads disinformation."

"But, he's no longer the landlord," said Michael, "so why should he care?"

"If he could panic the shareholders," explained Moscowitz, "then he could force the building into foreclosure and pick it back up for a song. He could have his cake and eat it. At least that's my theory. The murders do fit into that plan."

"There's no percentage in murder," said Archie. "It's one thing to yell at a tenant or set a little fire to your own property. You get their respect that way. But murder? Too many hassles."

"Your whole life here has been a lie, Archie," said Michael, "how can we believe you now?"

As Archie was coaxed outside toward the convoy of patrol cars, Michael found himself relating the Archie story over and over. Moscowitz stayed at the doorman's station and made entries in his notebook. He did not even look up when the police convoy sped off.

Where's Dolores, Michael wondered.

His eyes searched the lobby until they found Dolores walking with Roberta Haven toward the elevator. He broke away from the small group, and rushed over to the two women.

"I'm going to look at Roberta's flower photos," Dolores told Michael.

She seemed to be saying something else; but he couldn't make it out.

"Excuse me?" he asked.

"I didn't say anything," said Dolores.

She covertly pointed to her lips, and moved her lips; but he still couldn't hear anything.

"What?" he asked.

She rolled her eyes, and exaggeratedly moved her lips.

Her and her lips, he thought. Lips. Lip reading.

He stared once more, and realized she was mouthing the words, "Get me in fifteen minutes."

Dolores and Roberta were in the elevator; the door closed; and Michael returned to his task as the teller of the story of Archie. He wondered why Moscowitz was still in the building.

When Michael punctually arrived at Roberta's door and knocked, there was no answer. He knocked again. He heard a few footsteps, a pause, and then more footsteps. Michael saw Roberta peering through the peephole.

Why does she invite people to visit her, thought Michael, if she wants to be left alone?

A phrase popped into his head as the door crept open: Leave lovers alone.

Roberta Haven stood in her apartment's dark hallway and smiled.

"Hello, Mr. Levine," she said.

"Hi, Roberta," said Michael, "I came by to remind Dolores that she has an appointment she has to keep."

Roberta stared at Michael's face for a moment.

"Oh," she said. "She mentioned something about that to me, but said she changed her mind, and wanted to stay here longer."

"Do you know how long she'll be?" asked Michael.

"I'm so sorry, Mr. Levine; but I really don't."

"Well, then, I'd better talk to her."

"That may not be possible, now. She's – uh – indisposed."

Michael smiled at Roberta's reluctance to utter such gross terms as "the bathroom."

"I'll wait," said Michael.

"Are you sure?" asked Roberta.

"Yes."

"Perhaps, you had better come in."

Roberta opened the door wider to give Michael entrance. He followed her into the dining room where she gestured toward an empty chair that matched the maple table. Michael dutifully sat.

214

"We had some tea," said Roberta. "Would you like some?"

Oh no, thought Michael, I hate tea but how can I be rude to Roberta?

"Thank you," said Michael, "That would be wonderful."

Roberta disappeared. Michael surveyed the dining room.

A loaf of cranberry bread and a knife were on the table. A placemat showing a field of tulips sat primly in front of Michael. As his eye moved about, Michael noticed a familiar calculator on a copy of *Reader's Digest*.

Michael felt a sudden chill.

Roberta carried a tea service on a gold lacquered tray to her dining room table. The teapot and mugs were pale gray with a light green reed design.

"Here you are, Mr. Levine," said Roberta. "Would you care for a piece of cranberry bread?"

"Is that Herman's calculator?" Michael asked.

"Why yes," replied Roberta, "I suppose it is."

Roberta sliced the cranberry bread with an economy of motion. She carefully placed the symmetrical slice on a lemon yellow paper napkin.

"Thank you," said Michael.

Roberta sat opposite Michael.

"Do you know, Mr. Levine," she said, "this may not be a proper thing for me to say; but I have always admired your manners."

"That's very kind of you," said Michael. "I try to have good manners; but I can't take credit for them. That's just how my parents trained me. Sometimes I think my manners get in my way, and I wish I could be more direct."

"Oh, no," said Roberta, "you must never feel that way. Good manners are so important."

Michael's eyes again traveled the room, and he noticed Dolores's unzipped camera bag on an upholstered piano stool. He could see that the camera's back was wide open, and no film was in the camera.

"I should see what's keeping Dolores," said Michael.

"I believe she had a slight stomach discomfort, but I'm sure she'll be right back."

"I don't think she likes anybody to touch her cameras."

"I understand," said Roberta. "I feel the same about my tools; but I couldn't let anybody see a picture of me and that nice young man in the garden. Some things are supposed to be secrets. It's not nice for a lady to express herself physically."

"Herman Matterweil," said Michael, recalling Herman's file of anguished correspondence, "wouldn't leave lovers alone."

"That's right," said Roberta. "He was always making rules about who could come into the building, and who couldn't. Things became uncomfortable when he discovered my little weakness. We call things 'private' for a reason. I simply cannot endure the thought of anyone being in possession of my secrets. Anyone! Do you understand what I'm saying, Mr. Levine?"

She means me and Dolores, he thought.

"I think so."

"Mr. Matterweil thought he could benefit from my secret. But I showed him the error of his judgment."

"What about Blanche Copra?" asked Michael.

"Another person with rules. She wanted to know everybody's business. There are things a lady must do that are nobody's business. She saw me with a nice young man. She spied on me. And you know even after I closed her eyes, she still kept looking at me. I hit her and hit her and she still could see my secret. Things are getting so complicated.

"I just can't help myself," continued Roberta as her strong hand slipped toward the knife that had just cut the cranberry bread. "I've tried; but a nice young man comes along, and I get so weak. Everybody has to be secret about something. This has to be my secret."

Michael quickly stood. Keeping his eyes fixed on Roberta, he backed away toward the hallway.

She lunged toward him.

Again with a knife, thought Michael, as he dodged Roberta. He kept edging back, and was now in the living room. His legs hit something – a coffee table. He toppled backward. Roberta jumped onto him. He pushed back and felt some unrecognizable part of her body. It felt strong. The hand, wrapped tightly around the knife, arced toward him. He thrust his right arm out, and managed to knock the knife out of her hand.

Roberta placed her hands on his throat and squeezed. Michael tried to push her away but felt her grasp tighten.

The doorbell rang but Roberta, disregarding good manners, continued to squeeze.

The doorbell rang again, followed by an impatient knocking.

I wish she'd answer the door, thought Michael. I'm giving in. I see an angel. She looks like—

"Hey," shouted Dolores.

Roberta glanced over her shoulder. Michael seized the moment's hesitation to flail out. Roberta held on. Michael noticed the warm aroma of Roberta's perfume.

How sweet, he thought.

He saw that Dolores had raised her hands. They were over her head, almost behind her, and then they swiftly came forward bringing a blur of color with them. Michael heard a thud. Roberta's hands relaxed, and her body went slack as it slumped to the right. Resting beside her was Dolores's weapon, an oversized edition of *Audubon's Birds of North America*. A spot of blood on her scalp showed where the book made contact.

"Are you all right?" asked Dolores.

"I thought she poisoned you," said Michael.

Outside the apartment, a shoulder slammed at the front door.

"She might have," said Dolores. "I think it was just something mild to take me out while she decided what to do with me. My system got rid of it."

Shoulder slam number two worked.

"Could you see who's at the door?" asked Michael.

It was Moscowitz. He looked at Michael, then Dolores, then the reclining and slightly bloodied Roberta.

Oh wait a minute, thought Michael. He thinks that we—

"She did it," said Michael, "and she's the one who wrote that note about lovers."

"I know," said Moscowitz, reaching for his handcuffs, "I came here to question her about it."

"You'll find Herman's calculator on the dining room table," said Michael

"This is some building you have here," said Moscowitz.

"Be it ever so humble," replied Michael.

THIRTY-FOUR

Big, Big Difference

Michael ambled through SoHo on the first Saturday of June. He was going to the opening of Dolores Caruso's exhibit. It was one of those pre-summer days when SoHo sparkles. The sun's rays bounced off brashly-painted walls and glistening plate-glass windows. People wore sillier than usual smiles as they fancy-stepped in and out of galleries, shops and restaurants. The day was ripe with delirium.

It was hard to realize that the Olmsted Court murders had taken place only a few weeks earlier.

Poor Roberta, thought Michael. She only wanted to be loved; but she couldn't accept the idea it was okay to love and be loved. She worried about what people might think of her. I have that trait; but I'm working on it. Why should considering thoughts and feelings of others be a bad trait? If it leads to homicide that's a sure sign something isn't working.

The photo gallery overflowed with people ready to celebrate the Ozarks or Dolores or photography or, at least, the availability of cheap white wine and cheese cubes.

Two aging, long-haired men, both wearing black shirts and jeans, stood perilously close to the cheese tray.

"I've been documenting the corporate subculture lately," said the stouter of the two.

"Oh," said the other, "I thought you were doing annual reports."

"That's what gave me the idea."

"Excuse me," said Michael.

The two stared at him.

"I want some cheese."

They stepped to the side and stared as Michael spooned cubes onto a paper napkin.

"What's the difference between your annual report work and the documentary project?" the slimmer man asked.

"Big difference," said the stouter photographer, "Big, big difference. I do the reports in color, and the documentary work is black and white.

The second long-haired man nodded significantly.

"Excuse me, again," said Michael.

"What?" asked the slimmer man.

"Do you know where Dolores Caruso is?"

The heavier man rolled his eyes, and pointed to a splash of blue across the room. As Michael pushed his way through the crowd, he heard one of the two men say, "He isn't anybody. Is he?"

"Are you kidding," said the other. "Did you get a load of those shoes?"

What, thought Michael, is wrong with my shoes?

Suddenly, Michael reversed course and caught up with the two photographers.

"Hey," he said, "what the hell is wrong with my shoes?"

"Excuse me?" asked the stouter photographer.

The slimmer one smirked.

"You made a remark about my shoes."

"Nobody really cares about your shoes," said the first photographer.

Michael gave the photographer what he hoped was a menacing glare.

"That's better," said Michael. "Let's keep it that way."

I must be crazy thought Michael. I almost got into a fight over shoes. Nope. It's not crazy to stick up for oneself or one's shoes, for that matter.

Suddenly, a vision in a blue jumpsuit embraced him.

"Oh, Michael," said Dolores, "I'm so glad you're here."

They kissed.

"I didn't realize this was such a big deal," said Michael.

"Oh it's nothing."

A thin, dark-haired woman with shiny brown eyes appeared at Dolores's elbow.

"Woody Bartholomew is eager to talk with you," said the thin, brown-eyed woman.

"Is he going to buy anything?" asked Dolores.

"Yep! So let's not keep him waiting too long."

"Sure," said Dolores, "but first, Colette I want you to meet Michael."

Michael and Colette shook hands. Her grip was firm and cold.

"Oh hi," said Michael, "you work here, do you?"

"You can say that," said Colette. "This is my gallery."

"Stay here," said Dolores to Michael. "I'll be right back."

As the two women walked away, Michael heard Dolores say, "isn't he precious?" But he couldn't hear Colette's reply.

Michael felt himself jostled.

It was Louis Irving.

"So what do you think about your photographer?" Irving asked.

My photographer, thought Michael. Sounds good.

"I'm impressed," he said.

"Face it, Levine, your sweetheart is a star."

"Louis," Michael began, "do you think there's anything wrong with my shoes?"

Louis glanced at Michael's feet.

"Nahh, they're just plain old shoes."

"They're not really that old," said Michael.

"Why am I critiquing your shoes?"

"Sorry," said Michael. "These two guys made a remark about them, about me, really."

"They shouldn't be worrying about your shoes. They should be worrying about the man who has no shoes."

At just this moment, Dolores reappeared.

"Sorry Michael, I had to take care of some business."

"That's okay."

"It's better than okay," said Dolores. "I just sold three images."

"Congratulations," said Michael.

"That's wonderful," said Louis Irving. "Remember me?"

"Of course," said Dolores. "You live in Michael's building. How are you?"

"Are you having a good time?" Dolores asked Michael.

"You're a star," said Michael.

Dolores actually giggled

"No it's true," said Michael. "Louis made me aware of it. And he never lies."

"I," said Louis, "speak truth to power."

"You are both very sick people," said Dolores.

"Boy," said Louis, "she's got your number."

"Oh-oh," said Dolores. "Colette is waving me over. It's back to work for me."

Michael grabbed Dolores's left hand.

"Louis also called you my sweetheart. I like that."

"He might even be right," said Dolores. "Stick around."

Michael smiled as he watched Dolores wade into the crowd.

"I haven't seen you since that little tsimmis in Olmsted Court," said Louis.

"The murders? A little tsimmis?"

"Oh we'll be talking about it for years," said Louis, "But it's not even a footnote in the people's history book. Although I did tell you Calvin was innocent. Did I not?"

"I know," Michael, "truth to power."

"Works like a charm."

"You know what else works like a charm?" asked Michael.

"What?"

"Defending your shoes against all enemies – foreign and domestic."

"If you say so," said Irving.

"I do," said Michael.

About the Author

Norman Schreiber got his start as a young playwright; he trained with Samson Raphaelson, Group Theater alumnus Wendell K. Phillips, and director Gene Frankel.

When director Robert Downey, Sr. first clapped eyes on Norman, he cast him as the homicidal messenger in *Putney Swope*, the uproarious, notorious indie film classic.

5,896,399 gazillion magazine articles, short stories, three books, some plays and a rock musical later, Norman Schreiber writes about music, travel, media, photography, small business and pop culture, and is the editor of Travelersusanotebook.com.